ALANA OAKLEY

T0282793

TORMENT & Trickery

An imprint of Enslow Publishing

WEST **44** BOOKS™

Please visit our website, www.west44books.com.
For a free color catalog of all our high-quality books,
call toll free 1-800-542-2595 or fax 1-877-542-2596.

Cataloging-in-Publication Data
Names: Inkwell, Poppy.
Title: Torment and trickery / Poppy Inkwell.
Description: New York : West 44, 2020. | Series: Alana Oakley
Identifiers: ISBN 9781538384831 (pbk.) | ISBN 9781538384824 (library
bound) | ISBN 9781538384848 (ebook)
Subjects: LCSH: Detective and mystery stories. | Arson--Juvenile fiction. |
School--Juvenile fiction. | High school students--Juvenile fiction.
Classification: LCC PZ7.I559 To 2020 | DDC [F]--dc23

Published in 2020 by
Enslow Publishing LLC
101 West 23rd Street, Suite #240
New York, NY 10011

Cover design and Illustrations: Dave Atze

Typesetting: Think Productions

Printed in the United States of America

CPSIA compliance information: Batch #CS19W44: For further information contact
Enslow Publishing LLC, New York, New York at 1-800-542-2595.

ALANA OAKLEY

TORMENT & Trickery

An imprint of Enslow Publishing

WEST **44** BOOKS™

by Poppy Inkwell

For five more reasons why the world is
an extraordinary place...

Kylie, Kelvin, Stuart, Meg, and Cailean

ACKNOWLEDGMENTS

While editing this book I had a car accident. I was very lucky and walked away with only a broken arm and wrist. A couple of scenes in the book treat road accidents rather casually – I use humor as a tool and it is deliberately absurd and over-the-top – so allow me this opportunity to be serious for a minute...

Speed kills./Real mates don't let mates drink and drive./Be alert don't get hurt./Stop. Revive. Survive./Drive now. Text later.

We all know the safety slogans and after being in a REAL accident I can tell you that there is NOTHING funny about them. So please, please, please, stay safe and where possible, keep your loved ones safe, too.

To this end, I'd like to **T**hank all of the extremely **H**eroic men and women of the police force and accident and emergency services. It takes real guts to turn up to work every day not knowing what strife people have gotten themselves into. As well, the **A**mazing orthopedic doctors, nurses, and surgeons of Nambour Hospital who kept me pain-free and then spent 5½ hours fixing my wrist – I'd give you a thumbs-up but we all know that radial nerve damage prevents me from doing it. Thanks in advance to the physiotherapists and osteopaths who will help me achieve that goal. Next, thanks to the **N**oble teachers who supported my family and me while I was incapacitated. My **K**indest friends and family deserve special mention also. All the wonderful people who helped me look after the children until their dad returned, Allison, Cheri, Jacqui, Jason, and Todd, but most especially the Wilson family who took us in after the dreaded call: To Nick for his awful puns, to Kerri for taking it all in her stride, to Alice for her wicked humor (Q: How do you get Poppy out of a tree? A: Wave), to Sophia whose free spirit is a thing of wonder and beauty. And PJ for being PJ. Last, but not least, the **S**elfless strangers, those anonymous Good

Samaritans who helped untangle my arm from the steering wheel, held my hand, kept me calm, and convinced me that I'd look much cooler with my new scar. Thank you Bro "Dreads," Dr. "Moon," and Mrs. "Heart" for being my guardian angels for the day.

THANKS!

Alana Oakley

CONTENTS

fate/feĭt/*n.* *& v.* −*n.***1** a power regarded as predetermining events unalterably. **2 a** the future regarded as determined by such a power. **b** an individual's appointed lot. **c** the ultimate condition or end of a person or thing. **3** death, destruction. **4** (usu. **Fate**) a goddess of destiny, esp. one of three Greek or Scandinavian goddesses.

[The Australian Concise Oxford Dictionary, 1993]

PROLOGUE

Fate.

What did it *really* mean?

If Alana had worn blue laces instead of neon, if her bike had had a flat, or if she'd stepped in gum (the stubborn, sticky kind) and been delayed five minutes picking it off, then maybe, just maybe, she wouldn't have met the "tall, dark, mysterious stranger," as Sofia's cousin predicts. Or uncovered his secret …

Secrets … sometimes they conceal something fiendish and deceitful, and other times something truly miraculous.

A thousand random moments. A thousand different choices. A thousand different outcomes.

Was it fate?

Alana didn't know, but she *did* know things were not always what they seemed.

CHAPTER 1

New boy on the block

Alana Oakley parked her bicycle on the grounds of Gibson High. A few older students, some of whom she didn't know, waved as they passed the girl whose long, normally dark, flyaway hair contained a new streak of plum. It was tied back in a high ponytail with neon shoelaces. Alana smiled broadly, the dimples which she'd inherited from her father, Hugo, deepening in reply. It was great to be in Year Eight and no longer at the Bottom of the Food Chain. It also helped that last year Alana and her friends won the Original Song Contest, scoring tickets and backstage passes to see Slam Guru and Jet Tierbert, two of the world's hottest music acts. That she'd reportedly shown teen heartthrob Jet "a thing or two" on the guitar after the concert had set school tongues wagging and eyes agog.

"Lana!" three voices called out at once. Alana's dark ponytail swung in response and she broke into a grin. Alana's closest friends, Khalilah, Maddie, and Sofia, bounced over to her. Khalilah, plumper than the other two, lagged slightly behind. Alana admired Sofia's new yin and yang pendant, even though it was hard to see amongst the plethora of lucky charms she still wore.

Maddie's sea-colored eyes sparkled with good humor as she teased their friend. "I thought you'd given up all that superstitious stuff for Hard Science?"

Sofia flicked back her hair – now dreadlocks, dyed three different shades of purple – and laughed. "I already told you. It can't hurt, right? And with Coach Kusmuk for P.E., I need all the luck I can get."

"I heard a rumor she was leaving the school," Alana said hopefully.

"Not this year," Sofia said with a crestfallen face. All the same, she gave her lucky Medallion of Hopeless Causes a determined rub.

The other girls groaned. Not Coach Kusmuk again!

Khalilah slung an arm around her friend's shoulders. "I've been thinking about that, Maddie, and I've got a great idea," she began, but everyone was already shaking their heads an emphatic "No." They knew all about Khalilah and her Great Ideas. Who else would have thought of trapping last year's Magic 8 Ball thief with "unwet" water, drenching the P.E. teacher in the process?

"You know my cousin, Erin, the psychic?" said Sofia. None of them did, but they nodded anyway. "She came over last weekend and said a tall, dark, mysterious stranger would be entering our lives," she declared dramatically. Before Sofia could explain further, a group of girls in their year clustered around. Soon everybody was chatting animatedly about music, teachers, and their schedule. Younger students stood on the fringes in awe.

The Year Sevens were soon herded away for a formal welcome by Gibson High's acting principal, Mr. Turner. Alana and her friends remembered his speech from last year. No doubt the new batch of Year Sevens would also be urged to "explore, experiment, and enjoy" by the rotund, rosy-cheeked man students good-naturedly dubbed "Santa."

A quick glance at the school calendar in their planners revealed some striking differences to last year: "Shakespeare Week" in April sounded intriguing. So did the new elective, "Foreign Languages." One thing that hadn't changed was the mid-year exams in July, which Alana hoped would not be too stressful. It looked like their game against the Soccer Academy was scheduled around the same time. With their new team, they had a real shot at winning. Alana began mentally calculating how many soccer practice sessions they could fit in before the match.

"So what did you choose for Foreign Languages?" Khalilah said, interrupting Alana's thoughts. Alana's friends knew she was trying to learn French in memory of her father, Hugo, who had died four years ago. French, however, wasn't offered. With the government drive to be economically competitive in the Asia-Pacific region, the girls could choose between Mandarin and Malay. The choice was a no-brainer for Khalilah, who was Bruneian.

"I chose Mandarin," Alana began, but broke off when the other three cried in protest.

"How could you not do Malay, Alana?" Khalilah cried, clearly disappointed. "I thought we could hang out at my house to study. Dad even offered to teach us how to make *rendang*."

Alana felt a pang of remorse. The girls had discussed the two options when the letter about electives arrived before the end of Year Seven. Although Khalilah's dad *did* make the best *rendang* curry, she'd been swayed into taking Mandarin by Auntie Ling Ling from Singapore, who had offered to help. Maybe she should have thought twice about the offer. This *was* Auntie Ling Ling, after all: co-mastermind of disasters like her mom's full-body tattoo (which almost happened) and smuggling Auntie Katriona into Slam Guru's concert as a "Sekurity" Guard (which did happen).

OMG! Could she have made the biggest mistake of her school career?

Alana shook off the negativity. This was not the right frame of mind to start the first day of school. "I'm sorry," she said with real regret. "The subject description said we'd get to do calligraphy painting." Khalilah continued to pout. "I promise I'll be there for the cooking demo though," she said, flipping her backpack high over her shoulder. "I adore your dad's curry!"

"*Oof*," Alana heard somebody wince. It was a boy. A new boy. And he was rubbing his chin where her bag had landed hard.

Alana glanced up and did a double take. The new boy was tall and lanky. Most of the buttons of his school shirt were undone and his tie was at half-mast. Dark, floppy bangs and scuffed shoes completed the look. But it was his eyes which grabbed Alana's attention the most. They were a curious shade of gray. Like rainclouds on a stormy day. At this moment they were glaring back as the boy checked for the smudge that must be on his nose. Alana realized with a start that she was staring. Her friends nudged each other, whispering. Was this the tall, dark, mysterious stranger Cousin Erin had foretold? If so, he was really cute! In many ways he reminded them of the teen pop star, Jet Tierbert. But while Jet exuded Rock Glam edginess, this guy took it further with an air of Bad Boy menace. They exchanged excited glances.

"Sorry," Alana mumbled, strangely tongue-tied.

The new boy shrugged. His eyes lost their stormy look, changing as swiftly as the elements they resembled. "Sure," he shrugged.

"Good to see you've met," boomed a voice that could only belong to Coach Kusmuk. "You and your friends can take our new student, Flynn, to science since you're in the same class. But don't try to experiment on him. If I recall," she said, turning to gaze at Khalilah, Maddie and Sofia, who'd taken a sudden interest in the clouds, "your 'experiments' don't have a high success rate."

The coach stalked away. Some people never forget, or forgive, and Coach Kusmuk was doing neither. It looked like last year's trick with "unwet" water still annoyed her. It didn't help Coach Kusmuk's mood that she had been mistaken for a school student (and a boy at that) again this morning. Her slight build – a legacy from her years as a world-class gymnast – and her androgynous features confounded staff, who still questioned her presence in the staffroom. It was a constant source of frustration.

Alana expected Mr. Murray, their usual science teacher with the too-tight trousers, to greet them first period with his habitual squat. Instead it was a substitute teacher, Miss Metcalf, a freckly figure with bleached blonde hair, who met them at the door. In her hand she had photocopied worksheets, which she gave to each student as they filed through.

"Hi everyone?" she said, once they'd quieted down. "My name is Miss Metcalf? I'll be taking you for science today because Mr. Murray is sick? He left you a worksheet to do which looks, like, *really* hard, so I'll let you get on with it?" She ended each sentence on a higher note so that it sounded as if she was asking rather than telling them. With a bright smile the teacher moved to her desk. Within minutes, she was logged on to her laptop checking for cheap flights. She'd heard the surfing in Northern Peru was exceptional this time of year.

Alana chose the seat next to Miller White after making sure the new student, Flynn, was settled. She needn't have worried. It was clear Sofia and Khalilah were taking Flynn under their wing. The two girls elbowed a couple of thickset boys out of the way to wedge Flynn between them. Sofia took a firm grip of Flynn's arm to show him a seat with Khalilah close behind. The three of them shuffled sideways like a crab as Flynn's feet dangled briefly above the floor. He ended up sandwiched between Sofia and Khalilah on a desk really meant for two. The girls beamed up at him. Sofia's mood ring had morphed into a rich burgundy, while Khalilah shot Flynn the kind of glances she usually reserved for cream buns. Alana turned to exchange a knowing look with Maddie, only to find Maddie cradling her chin and staring at him too with a dreamy expression on her face! Uh-oh! Alana didn't know if Flynn was the "tall, dark, mysterious stranger" they were predicted to meet, but she didn't have to be a psychic to know that Flynn was Trouble.

Alana slid into her seat. It was part of her New Year's resolution to try to do something different every day, and Miller White was definitely Something Different. Alana thought Miller might have had to repeat because he was kind of slow. Or seemed to be. He took things literally, which made conversation tricky. It didn't help that he wore odd-shaped glasses to accommodate eyes that were spaced far apart, like fried eggs sliding off the sides of his face.

Alana didn't understand the video game obsession Miller shared with his friends, but as Uncle James was always reminding her, things were not always what they seemed. James ... Alana sighed. She missed him when he was working on photo shoots in exotic locations. He and her mom were a great team – every time Emma interviewed the Rich and Famous, the celebrated photographer was there to get the perfect shot. Alana had a real love for photography too, and this shared passion had drawn them closer, especially with her dad gone. They'd taken to exchanging pictures with the new smartphone James had finally bought. On impulse, Alana checked her phone in case James had posted a photo. He had! *My impression of a gorilla's nostrils,* she read. Alana stifled a laugh. James had taken a close-up of his nose. *The real thing,* said the next tag. Alana marveled at how regal and breathtaking the female gorilla was. James had captured the intelligence and curiosity which shone from the primate's eyes, head cocked to one side. Alana checked no one was watching before sneaking the phone up to her own face. She flared her nostrils and zoomed in to take a photo to send back to James. Oops: from the corner of her eye she could see Miller gawking. She hoped someone had warned *him* things were not always what they seemed.

While Alana was working hard at getting a non-blurry close up of her nose, and Miller was working hard at not staring because it was rude, Miss Metcalf was working equally hard at doing no work at all. But today things were not going as planned. Within ten minutes, most of the students had finished the task and were looking for something else to do. They were looking for more work. They were looking to be taught! She was appalled. What was wrong with them? Didn't they have balls of paper to throw at each other? *Kids these days have no imagination or initiative!* she lamented.

Miss Metcalf spied a television in the corner. She checked her watch. Perfect timing! *Speedsters,* a live program televising high-speed car chases from around the world, was on. It was very educational. Hadn't Julie Metcalf herself learned to do a 180-degree turn from watching the show?

Alana raised her hand. "Umm, Miss Metcalf? What does *Speedsters* have to do with science?"

Khalilah, Sofia, and Maddie looked at her with amazement. They were only allowed to watch daytime TV when they were sick at home. What was Alana complaining about?

The new boy, Flynn, turned to stare too. Eyes the color of cold steel bored into her. What was this girl's problem? A teacher was letting them watch the coolest show on Earth and she was questioning its educational merits?

"S-q-u-a-r-e," he mouthed at her, miming the shape with long, spidery fingers.

Alana ignored him. She didn't care for him or his opinions, even though her friends clearly thought otherwise. Although it was only his first day, Flynn instantly made himself popular by pointing out the physics principles of a well-executed wheelie.

Chapter 1

"Miss," Flynn protested. "We could learn about Newton's third law of motion by watching *Speedsters*. There are lots of wheelies on the show, right?" The substitute teacher nodded vigorously. Flynn, encouraged, continued his explanation. "Newton said that for every action, there is an equal and opposite reaction." A vacant look passed across the substitute teacher's eyes. To her relief, Flynn went on. "So the main reason you can do a wheelie is because the axle is trying to spin the tires. As the axle turns the wheels forward, there's an *equal and opposite reaction*, which tries to make the axle turn in the opposite direction. I'm sure there's an equation or something to go with it," Flynn waved his hand vaguely in the air.

"$Wd = Fh$," Miller muttered.

Flynn snapped his fingers. "That's it. $Wd = Fh$! Where W ...?" he looked to Miller for help.

"Is the weight of the car," Miller supplied.

Flynn urged him on, "and d is the ..."

"... horizontal distance between the center of gravity and the rear axle ..."

Flynn's fingers gestured impatiently, "and F is ..."

"...the traction force at the rear tires and h is the center of gravity height," Miller said in a rush.

Alana stared at Miller in amazement. She had been wrong about him. Completely.

"Exactly!" Flynn pumped a fist in the air and then held out his hand to Miller for a high five. Miller gave Flynn's palm a blank stare.

Sofia took the opportunity to read the lines of Flynn's palm. "Romance," she said breathily. "I see romance." Flynn extracted his hand from Sofia's and edged away. He ended up closer to Khalilah, a move which made Khalilah's smile widen.

The teacher turned up the volume with a smirk. "So there," Alana could almost hear Miss Metcalf add silently to the argument.

The car chase that was live-to-air did not disappoint viewers. A battered car sped down the highway on the wrong side of the road, ten police cars in tow. The *thwuk, thwuk, thwuk* of a helicopter above added to the drama. Road blocks were set up, but the car continued its high-speed flight. People's thighs pressed into the edge of seats. Necks craned forward. What would the car do?!

Alana felt a tingle, almost a shiver, in the back of her mind. The aging car shouldn't have looked familiar. But it did. Alana's stomach tightened. She watched in growing horror as a line of policemen waved their hands. The car sped on. Closer. Closer. With a frantic look left and right, police officers dived out of the way seconds before the barriers behind them smashed. *Strike!*

Any social prestige Alana had gained for winning the Original Song Contest, tickets, and backstage passes to the hottest concert, and meeting the one boy every girl in school had a poster of, disintegrated when the *Speedsters* camera zoomed in. On her *mother*! Alana tried very hard to disappear into her chair.

"Get-out-of-the-car-with-your-hands-up!" Officer Henley yelled. The gun in his outstretched hand trembled. In fact his entire body was trembling, from the top of his sunburned ears to the tips of his black buffed shoes. Then and there, Officer Henley made a promise to himself: as soon as he finished making this arrest he was going to eat pancakes topped with marshmallows, chocolate sauce, sprinkles, golden syrup, whipped cream, *and* butterscotch ice cream. Life, he'd just realized, was too short not to.

The camera wobbled as it jogged into place, just catching Emma Oakley before she fell flat on her face with a wobbly *"Yee-ha!"*

"Isn't that your mom, Alana?" Miller said.

Flynn's eyes widened as he watched her squirm. *Your mom?* the new boy's shocked expression seemed to say.

CHAPTER 2

Social death

Although Alana and her mom looked very alike, with the same almond-shaped eyes and dark, brown hair which seemed to have a mind of its own, it was there that the similarities ended. Emma's idea of a Good Time, for example, was to hire a real crocodile for Alana's pirate-themed birthday party, dancing llamas that couldn't dance, and fire breathers that set fire to Alana's hair. For everybody in the southern hemisphere, the first of September marked the first day of spring. For Alana it meant an annual trip to the hospital. With her dad, Hugo, gone, Alana was the one who made sure their bills were paid on time and that important dates were remembered. Somebody around the house had to.

It was no surprise, then, that Emma followed her own logic when it came to recipes, D.I.Y., and medical prescriptions. More jelly? Simple: add another cup of boiling water. Botched job above the fireplace? Easy: cover the hole with a mirror. Sick? No problem: just take four times the dose of painkillers to get better, *four times faster.* She had an article to finish and a deadline to meet. Emma wasn't wasting time nursing a sore tooth. And there was no way she was going to a dentist! Earlier that morning (before her debut on *Speedsters*) she'd lined up the bottles of herbal remedies, anti-histamines, and painkillers her friends, Katriona and Ling Ling, had provided, and popped one of each into her mouth. With cheeks bulging like a hamster, she kissed Alana goodbye, before getting in her battered car. As an afterthought, she jotted an idea for her article on the car window in peach lipstick.

Emma drove the way she lived life – straddling two lanes at the same time, as if she couldn't decide which direction to take until the last minute. When the chemical concoction began to take effect, passing cars seemed to slow down, while traffic lights rocketed into the air. Everything felt muddled. Psychedelic colors spun. Emma experienced a sudden rush of energy. She pushed her foot on the accelerator. *Wheeee!* She could fly!

Drivers were terrified by the car's erratic behavior.

"Watch out!" an ambulance driver yelled, when the car overtook him.

"Maniac!" cried a Maserati driver as Emma flew past.

In answer, Emma gave a royal wave and smiled serenely. Through the hazy fog that was now pain-free, she sang: "Rubber ducky, you're the one. You make bath time so much fun. Rubber ducky, you're the one for meeeeeee!"

The car jumped over a barrier and landed hard, jerking like a bucking bronco. "*Woh*, Nellie," Emma responded. She stroked her "horse." The steering wheel spun out of control. Now the car was traveling 120 kilometers an hour, down a busy highway, *on the wrong side of the road*.

Drivers swore and swerved to avoid the car. Emma stared at them like they were wild steeds to be caught, her lips pulled back in a manic grin. She whipped her "horse" and urged it forward. The car wiggled all over the road. One by one, the car attracted a string of police cars like iron files to a magnet. Sirens blared. Lights flashed. Emma reached for her lasso …

…

When the charge against Alana's mom, Emmalina Estafania Corazon Oakley, was read aloud for Emma to respond to, no one was more surprised than her.

"I have no memory of it, Your Honor … ess," she added, because the judge was a woman. If the judge appreciated Emma's thoughtfulness, she did not show it. If anything, her expression became sterner. Judge Debnham's constant displeasure had worn grooves into the skin surrounding her mouth and between the two neatly plucked auburn eyebrows that hovered over piercing blue eyes. She did not suffer fools gladly. While the framed cross-stitch in her office warned: "Your sin will find you out," a common addendum to the saying was that if your sin didn't find you out, Judge Debnham most certainly would. Such was her reputation around the courts.

Judge Debnham's voice rang clear. "Your poor judgment came at great expense to the local taxpayer, Ms Oakley. High-speed car chases do not come cheap. Thankfully, no one was hurt, but I cannot let this pass without some lesson to be learned. According to your record, you have displayed several instances of misplaced judgment before. I hereby sentence you to a total of thirty hours community service, so the wealth of your … 'expertise' … can be shared with others less fortunate."

"Plead the Fifth!" came a voice from the back of the courtroom.

"We're not in America, you fool!" Katriona cried.

"America, Australia, same-same lah!"

"Who said that?" Judge Debnham demanded with a severe purse of her lips. A bout of angry whispering ensued.

After a few moments, Ling Ling stood up, resplendent in varying shades of orange. She was going through a "Buddhist phase" after a trip to Thailand. The saffron hues of the monks' robes had made an impression ... though not of the spiritual kind. A slipper of iridescent gold pressed firmly into the toes of the woman beside her until she too, jumped up with a glare. The woman was just as tall as Ling Ling but shaped like a sitar – thin and flat on top while her backside ballooned. While today, Ling Ling favored the rich, shimmering colors of the East, the other woman assumed the jungle print of a tiger. The fabric clung to her curves as if the pelt were her own. Black and orange striped nails gripped her waist as her not-so-sizeable chest leaned in one direction and her more sizeable rear took off in the other. She wasn't taking any chances – you never knew when someone might take a photo.

"Ahh yes, let me hazard a guess that one of you is Ms Katriona Karovsky and the other, Ms. Ling Ling Shu. You seem, Ms. Oakley, to persist with friends with whom you share a colorful past." The judge eyed her speculatively. "Obviously you're the type of person who takes longer to learn their lesson. Perhaps *forty* hours of community service is more appropriate? Unless counsel suggests otherwise?" she said with a pointed glance at Emma's friends.

"But she didn't know what she was doing." Alana burst out. "It was the drugs she took for her toothache!"

"And who may you be? Oh no, don't tell me. You must be Alana Oakley, the defendant's daughter. Thank you for your report cards, young lady, but I am afraid that straight A's do not change the fact that your mother broke several laws. And of course the charges only cover the infringements she was caught for. Who knows what else she might have done ..."

"But she didn't mean to!" James said next,

jumping up to stand next to Alana. James, back from his Ugandan photo shoot, looked lean and sun-tanned. Katriona immediately struck a new pose. *Raar!* she meowed, extending a claw to James. Surely he would be inspired to take a photo of her now? James's shocked eyes sought solace in the ceiling.

The judge leaned back in surprise and banged her gavel. "Enough! I will not have my court made a mockery of! I hereby sentence Emmalina Estafania Corazon Oakley to a total of *sixty* hours community service at the Police Boys' Club in Newtown. Perhaps *they* can have a positive influence on your life. And if I hear another word, I will make it eighty! IS. THAT. CLEAR?"

The sound of the gavel was loud and sharp. Any further protests died a quick death on people's lips. Judge Debnham paused and peered over her glasses.

"Have you seen to that tooth of yours yet, Ms. Oakley?"

Emma gulped. The air rushed from her lungs.

"Kind of …" she managed to choke out.

"May I remind you, you are under oath, Ms. Oakley. Either you have, or you haven't."

"Not yet, Your Supreme Highness."

"The court, therefore, also orders you to visit a dentist immediately. Well," she barked, "what are you waiting for?"

Emma stepped down from the witness stand and scrambled for her belongings before stumbling into the sun.

The dentist.

Emma's worst nightmare.

CHAPTER 3

A fall from grace

Alana sighed as she waited in line. She was stuck at Boot Camp (their new name for the gym) for another P.E. lesson filled with pain and suffering. Any hope that Coach Kusmuk had mellowed over the summer holidays faded as her yells bounced off the echoey walls. If anything, Coach Kusmuk had got worse. The rumor that she was transfering schools next year was all Alana's class could talk about.

"I heard she's being sent as a special consultant to deal with Childhood Obesity," Maddie huffed. "Childhood Obesity" was one of Coach Kusmuk's pet projects, as well as finding and seizing Inappropriate Items for her Confiscation Cupboard. Alana had seen firsthand the impressive collection of deviance accumulated over several generations.

"Yeah, that's all an overweight kid needs –

Coach Kusmuk yelling at them to go faster," Khalilah moaned in sympathy. Khalilah Madzaini fought with her weight the way you might fight with a phantom – with lots of useless punches at the air – but the "baby fat" remained stubbornly attached.

"Faster!" Coach Kusmuk yelled across the room.

Khalilah rolled her eyes. "See what I mean?"

"Just (*pant*) one (*pant*) more (*pant*) year," Alana promised, as she finished off her push-ups.

Everybody was engaged in a different training activity. Some were running a 60-meter sprint. Some were hanging from monkey bars on twisted towels slung over thin bars of steel. Others were doing flexed arm hangs, bench dips, push-ups, or balancing on a beam. "We're all going to die," Alana could hear Miller whimper as he looked at the set of tires he had to "tiptoe" through in under ten seconds. Students all over the gym dropped like flies.

The final activity was a wall climb. For

Khalilah, it felt like Mount Kinabalu. After only halfway up, she was struggling to go any further. The monkey bar exercise had ripped her arms from their sockets, and now the cargo net, was biting into her skin. She began to regret the extra doughnut for breakfast. She pulled upward with sweaty palms, then slipped back with a cry. Even though it was not yet her turn, Alana vaulted up the wall to whisper words of encouragement and lend a helping hand. But Coach Kusmuk's eyes in the back of her head did not appreciate the interference.

"If you think Khalilah can't complete the task, Alana, please don't let me stop you from helping her. In fact," she added with a nasty gleam in her expression, "since you and your friends like experimenting, let's conduct a little experiment of our own and see you *carry* Khalilah over the wall." Alana's face fell. One look at the coach's face told her she was not joking.

Alana squeezed under Khalilah until she had positioned her on her back. Khalilah did her best to help by alternately pulling and pushing off the cargo net with her hands and feet. That was until Coach Kusmuk shouted out the order to let go. Alana adjusted her body to shoulder the extra weight, and gripped the netting as she heaved. They inched toward their goal. Soon, Khalilah was not the only one regretting the extra doughnut. The class stopped to watch the girls' progress. Alana's back and calf muscles strained with each step. Her knees wobbled. Sweat collected on her forehead and dripped down her neck. Alana glanced at Coach Kusmuk who looked on in glee. She refused to give Coach Kusmuk the satisfaction of giving up. Alana gritted her teeth and pushed on. When they reached the top, there was a burst of applause. Khalilah raised Alana's hand in victory, but Khalilah's foot got stuck in the rope and she lost her balance, flinging Alana backward. Before Alana could regain her grip, she found herself tumbling to the floor in an untidy heap. Khalilah, meanwhile, was left hanging upside down. Her long plait swayed from side to side as her arms dangled like a rag doll. Even that reprieve did not last long as, with a sharp yell, she plummeted to land on top of Alana with a bone-crunching thud.

Coach Kusmuk tutted and placed doll-like hands on her narrow hips. "Hey, Flynn," she called out to the new boy, "take these two to the clinic, will you? They're done for now."

Flynn ambled over. He, of course, had had no difficulty with any of the activities. Alana shook off his helping hand with an impatient shrug, still smarting from her mom's embarrassing TV appearance. Khalilah, however, wrapped an eager arm around the boy's waist.

"I'll see you at kickboxing later. Don't be late this time," Coach Kusmuk warned Flynn as he helped Khalilah limp towards the door, Alana stubbornly hopping behind. It was only later, when the shock of being squashed had faded, that Alana realized what Coach Kusmuk had said. *Why was Flynn doing kickboxing, when it was only for Troubled Teens? Was New Boy a Troubled Teen, and if so, what was his crime …?*

…

"Snap! I win again!" Nurse Cathy put down her hand of playing cards when Alana and Khalilah hobbled in. "Ooh goodie, we've got company," she exclaimed.

Alana looked at the patients and shuddered. Last year there had been *one* patient wrapped in bandages from head-to-toe, like an Egyptian mummy. Now there were *two*! Patient Y sat next to a new Patient X, a pile of cards in front of each of them – the latest pair looked to be the victims of Nurse Cathy's well-thumbed volume of "A step-by-step guide to orthopedic care." Patient Y's body shape was shorter and rounder than its companion's. No one knew how long the new mystery patient had been in the clinic, although the lines scratched into the wall in groups of five gave some clue. Alana suppressed a tiny shudder.

The sight of them made Alana even more determined to play down her injury. It didn't pay to be sick at Gibson High.

It was only through some slick double-talking that Alana and Khalilah escaped the nurse's clutches with just a small bandage, a packet of painkillers, and an ice pack for swelling. They knew without looking that Nurse Cathy was gazing hungrily after them.

"Make sure you follow the dosage carefully, now," Flynn said to Alana with barely concealed mirth. "Wouldn't want to see your bike on *Speedsters*." With a wink he slouched away, hands in pockets, whistling.

Khalilah gave an appreciative chuckle, and then shrugged her shoulders at Alana's outraged expression. "What?" she said. "That was funny."

Alana gave an impatient growl and took off … with as much speed and dignity as hopping allowed.

CHAPTER 4

Say *Ahhh,* not *Arghhh*

The dental clinic was deserted. A receptionist in gloomy, tie-dyed satin and violet lace sat at the front desk. Dark, ghoulish makeup accentuated her pallid skin. Spots of funereal nail polish tripped over the keys of a computer in staccato. At Alana and Emma's approach, the young woman paused.

"Can I help you?" she said in a bored voice.

Emma moved forward reluctantly. "Ummm, Oakley. O-a-k-l-e-y. We have an appointment for 9 o'clock. But if you're busy, we're happy to reschedule."

Joy, the receptionist, looked up from her computer with dull eyes. She glanced around the still-empty room. "A joker, huh?" she said in a monotone. "Fill out the registration form. I'll need your contact details and medical insurance information."

"It was worth a try," Emma muttered as Alana complied with Joy's request and filled in the forms. Emma perched on the edge of a black leather lounge, one foot tapping nervously. She gazed around at the decor. The walls, furniture and flooring made up a monochromatic palette of blacks, whites, and grays. It was like walking into a newspaper comic strip. But Emma found nothing funny in what she saw. The only splash of color came from tiny, red fish housed in individual bowls, dotting stark white walls. *Why is it always fish?* Emma thought to herself, thinking of all the dental surgeries she'd been to … and run away from. Some had had big posters of "before" and "after" teeth, blackened with decay (before) and a disconcerting fluorescent white (after). Others had pictures of smiling toothbrushes telling jokes … *Q: Why do dentists like potatoes? A: Because they are so filling. Q: What's the best time to go to the dentist? A: Tooth-hurty. Q: What does a dentist call her X-rays? A: Tooth-pics.* However, the one thing the dental clinics had in common was a fish tank. As if the imprisoned creatures did nothing except remind her of how trapped she felt ... Emma found these particular modern furnishings cold and unwelcoming, and the fish, in their solitary confinement – *circling, circling, circling* – disturbing.

Emma, vegetarian and misguided animal lover, looked at them in dismay.

"Oh, you poor widdle fishies," she crooned. "I bet you're vewy, vewy lonely. Look, Alana," Emma said, holding up a bowl, "don't you think they look lonely?"

Alana, barely glancing up from a magazine, replied, "Put the fishbowl down, *Maman*," and continued to read. Alana often threw French words into her conversation. She tried to learn a new word or phrase every day. In a way she hoped that by speaking French she was keeping the memory of her father alive – a memory that, with every year that passed, felt more frayed and chewed at the edges.

Emma looked around the empty room and

crept sideways, careful not to spill the container she held. With a final check that neither Alana nor the receptionist was looking, Emma tipped the bowl until one tiny slip of color joined the other. "There you go," she said, "now you can make fwends."

"The doctor will see you now," the receptionist's voice called flatly.

Emma hastily returned the bowl and wiped wet hands on the seat of her pants. Alana, seeing the look of panic on Emma's face, took her mom's hand and led her into the room. Emma saw a figure in a white lab coat swivel in his chair. He stood up and held out a friendly hand. He was short. A thatch of dark hair was carefully slicked down with some kind of oil. He looked to Emma like the kind of person who trimmed his nasal hair, ate fiber-rich cereal, and drove under the speed limit. *I bet he's never been on Speedsters*, Emma thought irrationally. She shook the dentist's hand dumbly. To her panicked ears, his greeting sounded muffled, like he was speaking through a wad of foam.

Before Alana could protest, Emma pushed her daughter firmly into the dentist's chair. "Just a routine clean," she said, ignoring Alana's hazel-flecked eyes, which silently promised murder when they got home. Emma wasn't disobeying the court's ruling: she *was* visiting the dentist. That Alana was having the appointment was a minor technicality. Emma felt very proud of her solution.

"Well, if it's just a routine clean, why don't I get our lovely dental assistant to take care of you?"

The "lovely dental assistant" turned out to be Joy, now in a crisp, white overcoat of stiff, over-starched cotton which covered her Gothic garb. Above the face mask, Joy's lifeless eyes shone with sadistic delight as she looked into Alana's panicked ones. The chainsaw *buzz* of a dental machine started up. Emma couldn't suppress the shudder that ran through her body, and clamped a hand over her mouth. The dentist reacted instantly.

"Here," he said, leading her to a side office, "Can I get you some water?" He peered closer at her face. "Or a bucket?"

Emma accepted the glass gratefully and gave a self-conscious laugh. "You must think I'm an idiot."

"Not at all," he assured her. "Dentists scare a lot of people. Why don't you stay here until your daughter's treatment is finished?" And with that he walked out the door.

Twenty minutes later, Joy's less-than-joyful scream cut through the air. Emma raised her head from the plastic bucket in alarm and rushed into the waiting room. Where there had been two live fish in a bowl, now there was only one. The survivor's orbit now resembled a shark's. Alana glared at her mother. Any minute now she was going to say *Sorry, Terribly Sorry*, like she always did after causing trouble.

"Sor -" Emma began.

"Thank-you-we'll-be-going," Alana gabbled, snatching the invoice, grabbing her mother's hand,

and fleeing the room.

Their footsteps pounded the pavement as they ran to the car. "Fighting fish," Alana explained breathlessly.

CHAPTER 5

Torture in History

Within a few weeks Alana and her friends settled back easily into the routine of study and school work. Gibson High had not changed much. And Year Eight was the same as Year Seven, if slightly harder. They still had Mr. Hornby for math, with his obsession for morbid trivia, but for reasons unknown, Mr. Murray, with the too-tight trousers, never returned from sick leave for science. Miss Metcalf had discovered an abundance of photocopied worksheets, though, and always disappeared for a coffee during science lab – to the delight of Miller and his friends. Jack Stratt – or "Strut," as Alana called him – was on a country music tour, so Miss Beatrice, formerly a nun of the Benedictine Sisters from St. Bernadette's College, was taking them for choir.

A new subject for Year Eight was history, with a Mrs. Snell who had recently joined the school.

Mrs. Snell was an elderly woman who wore thick, thermal underwear, whatever the weather. The layers guarded her in equal measure against sudden drops in temperature and the threat of Peeping Toms. Neither of which was ever a concern. The *click, clack* of her knitting needles clattered in harmony with the smack of her dentures and the creak of her chair, which she liked to rock back and forth. Although Mrs. Snell looked to be as wholesome (and as harmless) as her apple-pie smile, experience soon taught Year Eight students otherwise. Her reputation spread throughout the school like wildfire. Within days of joining Gibson High, the gummy "great-grandmother" – strictly a figurative term – became one of the most feared teachers of the school. Even fellow staff quaked at the sight of her. Alana liked Gibson High for its progressive policies that allowed Sofia to have hair dyed three different shades of purple, a librarian who *didn't* use the Dewey system for filing books, and a school bakery run by the students themselves. But employing Mrs. Snell was Going Too Far. For their topic, "Tortures of the Eighteenth Century," there was consensus that everything Mrs. Snell taught them was true … *if only because she'd been there to administer it in person!*

New Boy, Flynn, didn't seem to care. He walked into all his classes with nothing but a pen, which he twirled expertly between fingers. He never used it for writing. As he slouched in his chair, the slim rod constantly wove itself into a blur. He could twirl it over his fingers, under his fingers, and side-to-side. Others tried to copy him but nobody could match his fluidity or speed. At the end of history, when the students had to hand in their first assignment on "Medieval Torture Devices," Flynn's hand shot up. His pen twirling like a baton in the air.

"Sorry, Mrs. Snell, but my dog ate it."

Immediately, a nervous titter danced around the class.

The knitting needles kept up a steady tempo.

"What was that, Dearie? Sometimes my hearing isn't very good."

Flynn was consulting what looked to be a Magic 8 Ball like Sofia's. It was, in fact, an Instant Excuse Ball. The kind you buy from novelty or joke shops, along with fart bombs and fake moustaches. It wouldn't have surprised Alana if Flynn had a stash of them, too. He sent a cocky look around the class as he read another excuse in a louder voice. "I can't hand in my homework because I was abducted by aliens."

Desks shuffled. Even Khalilah edged away.

"Speak up, please, Dearie. Old age is a terrible thing."

This time Flynn made no effort to hide the ball he was shaking. "Plus I had Mexican food last night …" he said, faking a groan and rubbing his stomach with a wink. A practiced belch erupted like an exclamation mark.

The class inhaled sharply.

Year Eight history – minus Flynn – was ushered from the room by the bell and Mrs. Snell's deceptively friendly smile. But a few of them, like Alana and her friends, hung back to see what would happen next. A low murmur was all they could hear. Silence. Then a short, high-pitched yelp. The kind a Chihuahua might make when it gets stepped on. By a ten-foot giant.

"Thank you, Dearie. I knew I'd heard wrongly. I look forward to reading your assignment over the weekend. 'Medieval Torture Devices' is one of my favorite topics," the elderly teacher said as she opened the door. The eavesdroppers scattered. A much more subdued Flynn walked out, pigeon-toed and shuffling. As he passed Alana and her friends, he gave his Instant Excuse Ball to Sofia.

"I won't need this anymore, you can have it," he wheezed, waddling away in obvious discomfort – but not before Alana caught sight of a deep imprint of a size-eight knitting needle in the middle of his forehead, and the top of his underpants sitting unreasonably high above his trousers.

Sofia gazed after Flynn, clutching the Instant Excuse Ball to her chest. "Don't you think Flynn is just the nicest guy?" she sighed.

Alana stared at her friend. She knew that look.

She'd seen it before. Usually worn by girls drooling over a Jet Tierbert poster.

Alana took Sofia's Magic 8 Ball charm in her hand, shook it, and showed her the answer.

Don't count on it, Sofia read.

CHAPTER 6

Teenagers, toddlers, same-same lah

Emma was nervous. She had never done any teaching before, yet somehow she was expected to help rehabilitate Troubled Teens. Not that they were called "Troubled Teens" anymore. Now they were referred to optimistically as "Second-Chancers" – even though for most of them this was their fourth or fifth "chance." Community service also meant a drastic change to her routine. Life, for the last four years since her husband's death, had consisted of getting up, researching on the computer, interviewing people – celebrities, politicians, activists – writing up an article, and then more research. If she managed to change out of her bedclothes, brush her hair, or eat for any of the time she wasn't interviewing, it was a miracle.

"No wonder you can't get a date," her friends, Katriona and Ling Ling, often moaned.

But to Emma, Getting A Date was not a top priority, much to her own mother's disgust. In Mrs. Corazon's eyes, now that a suitable mourning period had elapsed, it was high time Emma did the sensible thing and remarried – preferably someone nice, like Manny "Mandela" Manalog, or DOCTOR Manny Manalog, since he was an orthodontist now, you know.

It was a constant source of frustration to Emma that the only Nice Men her mother knew were doctors, lawyers, or dentists. Just the thought of going out with a man who spent eight hours a day with his fingers in other people's mouths was too gross to think about. She was perfectly happy with her life, thank you very much. Work was immensely satisfying, she had a wonderful daughter, and she had very good friends.

Alana didn't agree. In her opinion it couldn't be healthy to be so obsessed with work. Her mom burrowed into her job like a mole, and when she *did* bother to surface, her so-called "friends" were always getting her into trouble. Last year was a perfect example. Katriona and Ling Ling had set Alana's mom up on a dating website, where she began an online flirtation with *PeterPan,* who ended up being teen heartthrob, Jet Tierbert. That made Emma old enough to be his mother! Ewww! That was one birthday surprise Alana could have done without. What's more, they broke into the Sydney Aquarium, swam with dolphins, set off a fire extinguisher in the shark tank, and kidnapped a Little Penguin called Noodle. *But* they'd also held Emma's hand through the heartbreak of losing Hugo: months of walking around in a daze. *Gone. Gone forever.* The words had circled in Emma's brain until she thought she'd go mad.

It was no surprise that she turned to them again in this time of crisis.

"Look on the bright side," Katriona said matter-of-factly. "It'll be good for you to meet some new people. Maybe even some single dads," she winked. "Save a cute one for me," she added quietly with a wiggle of her shapely bottom.

Emma *tsked* as she popped another painkiller

in her mouth. A different brand this time, because the last one had turned her tongue blue. *And* caused an involuntary tick in one eye. Not exactly the first impression she wanted to make.

"Teenagers, toddlers, same-same lah," Ling Ling said before following Katriona in a floating flurry of sunburnt swirls. The beauty bar they ran offered complete makeovers (or "takeovers," as Alana called them) and their 2:30 was due. Ling Ling couldn't wait to transform their client into the beautiful woman she knew was hiding in oversized T-shirts and baggy pants.

Emma headed off to the first of her sixty hours of community service with those words of wisdom and an old copy of *Taming Your Tiny Two's*. She coaxed her battered car up to 15 kilometers an hour, ignoring the impatient toots and horns from the drivers behind her. Her car's debut on *Speedsters* had taken its toll. The car shuddered to a halt outside the Police Boys' Club with a wheezy cough. Emma took a deep breath. The moldy scent of old paper and baby puke that was the book's signature scent filled her nostrils, and she tried to stem the flood of memories it evoked.

Three youths meandered past her car. One wore a leather jacket that was too big for him and too warm for February. The jacket had the words "Crazy Mother" embroidered on the back. In the morning sunlight it was easy to see where a border of hearts and flowers had once been, by the tiny trace of holes they had left behind. Another boy – of Asian descent – was weaving up and down the pavement on a well-worn skateboard. He used the low brick wall by the club's entrance to attempt a Casper Slide, and landed head down and legs up, like a banana.

"Epic fail!" Leather Jacket jeered.

The third youth – a heavy-set boy whose low-seated pants were weighed down further by a monkey wrench in his back pocket – stretched his arms sumo-style to prevent the two from fighting. Emma couldn't see his face because he had his back to her, but his ears were the cauliflower kind that suggested a long history of playing some kind of rugby. That, and his lack of neck.

If that was the kind of people she was dealing with, Emma thought, she had better set some ground rules. Which is exactly what she did when she found herself in class in front of the same youths, fifteen minutes later. On the whiteboard provided by the administrator – who had simultaneously wished her "Good Luck" and whispered instructions on how to use the emergency exit – she began to write the words, "No bullying." Puzzlement painted faces a stormy black as the three youths struggled to read.

To cover his confusion, Boris, the boy in the oversized leather jacket, threw a wad of paper at the skateboarder, Trần's, face.

Trần protested. "Miss! Miss! This is disabl-ism!" He yelled, holding up a hand which had a thumb and only one finger. The story of how Trần lost the other three changed all the time. Some days he claimed it was a hunting accident. Other days, it was a kung fu move gone wrong. Whatever the reason, Two-Fingered Trần never hesitated to use the loss to his advantage. Enzo – the third boy – planted himself between the other two boys yet again in his peacekeeper's role. Thus it was that the two boys exchanged insults from a meter apart. Trần had the last word with what he called the "Trần Salute," by holding his L-shaped digits against his own forehead. "Loser!" he spat. Eventually, the room settled back down.

Emma pursed her lips, popped another painkiller in her mouth, and added *No swearing* and *No name-calling* to the list of rules, along with *No fighting.* As an afterthought, she underlined the additions and surrounded them with flowers and stars. Emma decided their first topic would be job seeking, for she was sure that somewhere, in some way, *somehow*, the Second-Chancers could make a positive contribution towards society. She just had to help them find it. They began with a role-play.

"Give me a job, or I'll bash yur head in!" demanded Boris. Boris looked at his peers, noting with satisfaction that they looked impressed.

Ling Ling was right. Teaching *was* a lot like bringing up a toddler. She quickly flicked through the book and found a passage which felt relevant. *Focus on the positive and praise them, while guiding the negative out the door.* "I love your directness, Boris (praising the positive), but I'm worried you're coming across too strong (guiding the negative out the door). Strength is a good thing, but we don't use our teeth to open a can of soda, do we?"

Not to be outdone, Boris tried again.

"Give me a job, or I'll bash your head in. Please."

A whistle of approval ran through the group.

Little steps, Emma promised herself as she rubbed her temples. *Little steps.*

CHAPTER 7

Two musical minds meet

Ex-Sister-now-Miss Beatrice of the Benedictine Sisters was a woman who loved God and music in equal parts, if only because she believed they were one and the same. If she were really honest, she loved "Musicals" and "Broadway" even more, and said a prayer of penitence whenever the thought stole into her mind. Thus Choir Class was an hour of singing *all the time*, even when the students only wanted to speak.

"Good morning, class," Miss Beatrice trilled at the start of every class.

"Good morning, Miss Beatrice," the class was expected to trill back.

Whenever anybody forgot and lapsed into the spoken word, she encouraged them with a dramatic wave of her arms, her frizzy hair bouncing in agitation. She reminded Alana of a heavy, flightless bird struggling for takeoff.

"Sing it. Sing it!" she would urge.

"I feel like a dork," Flynn breathed in a sing-song voice to Maddie, who giggled in spite of herself.

"Last week, we discussed dissonance and consonance," the teacher continued melodically. "In *Phantom of the Opera* the composer uses dissonance to evoke fear by combining notes that sound like they don't fit. Flynn and Maddie, could you please perform your composition on dissonance?"

"Yes, we can," Flynn answered in a deep, operatic voice, earning a huge smile from the teacher, and laughter from the class.

Maddie moved into position with her violin, sliding her bow along each of the strings to check she was in tune. Flynn made a huge show of exercising his lips before placing them experimentally on the mouthpiece of his saxophone. They nodded to each other and then there was an eruption of sound. A cacophony of notes clashed harshly. The noise made everybody wince.

"Lovely. Perfect. Now, consonance," Miss Beatrice sang with another wave.

"But we –"

"Sing it. Sing it."

Maddie tried again, singing, "We haven't prepared a piece for consonance."

But Miss Beatrice ignored their protests, urging them to find harmony in the musical scales they were familiar with. Maddie was a frequent user of social networking sites to meet other musicians, and she often jammed with friends online, so she was used to improvising. But would Flynn know what to do?

With a shrug, the pair resumed their positions and began, tentatively at first, and then with growing confidence, to feed off each other's sounds. If their music had been a painting, it would have filled the canvas with bold strokes of color. Up and down, the notes swirled. Flynn played a few bars from a classic sci-fi flick, which Maddie countered with a reference to a popular TV sitcom. The students laughed out loud. Sofia grabbed a couple of pens and began to drum the beat. Soon everybody, even Miss Beatrice, was tapping their hands and feet appreciatively, until the harsh sound of the bell interrupted Maddie and Flynn's melodic duet.

"Don't forget your homework on chromatic scales," Miss Beatrice sang as the students trooped out jauntily, the harmonies still ringing in their ears. "Wonderful work, you two," she aimed at Maddie and Flynn as they packed their instruments away.

"There are some deadly music websites I can show you if you want to do more of that stuff," Maddie said in a normal voice when they were out of the teacher's earshot.

"That would be great, thanks," Flynn said with a smile.

"Did you know, 83% of females polled last year said they thought the saxophone was the world's most romantic instrument?" Sofia informed her friends later.

"Not the *guitare*?" Alana said, surprised.

"I believe it," Maddie said dreamily.

Alana rolled her eyes. First Khalilah had succumbed to Flynn's charms. Then Sofia. Not Maddie, too?!

CHAPTER 8

A date with destiny

Emma dreaded Fridays. Every Friday, her mother called to find out how she was – although she never actually asked. Emma suspected she wasn't all that interested. Emma's mother spent most of the phone call providing information and updates about The Community – Filipino migrants like themselves who had moved in the hope for a better life: births and deaths, catastrophes and marriages … which were sometimes the same thing. That Emma had married a good-for-nothing-no-hope-bongo-drum-player-turned-famous-jingle-writer-who-had-passed-all-too-soon-God-rest-his-soul was an achievement she wore like a merit badge. But enough was enough. For the woman who bought her week's groceries with hoarded coupons, her daughter was a prime example of waste. It was time for Emma to get married again or, at the very least, begin dating. Preferably a Professional.

It was maddening that her only offspring should remain so stubbornly independent – not that Mrs. Corazon didn't try to convince Emma of the benefits of being otherwise.

She tried persuasion. "Dentists are such lovely people. So compassionate and caring."

Then bribery. "I bought you a beautiful pair of shoes to go with that dress I got for you last week. Two for the price of one, what a bargain! No, of course I won't wear it at the same time. It will look perfect for when you go out with Dr. Manny."

And when that didn't work, guilt. "My poor heart. You will kill me one of these days with your shenanigans. One day, you'll come home and find me as dead as a doorknob" – idioms weren't one of her strengths – "For my sake, you should think of settling down."

Now would *not* be a good time to confess that her latest "shenanigan" had landed Emma sixty hours of community service. With an ear half-cocked towards the high-pitched whine of her mother's prattle, Emma uttered the appropriate sounds for their Friday ritual – *Really? She didn't! You're kidding!* – while running an index finger along the Police Boys' Club dusty bookshelf. There had to be a better resource than *Taming Your Tiny Two's.*

Emma pulled a book from the shelf. It had a glossy cover wrapped around it and boasted over 200 pages of expertise on "teenage terrorists." Emma popped a painkiller in her mouth and backed into a wobbly office chair, still mumbling and *ooh-ing* and *ahh-ing* at the handset, which she'd now placed on speakerphone. She buried her nose in the book and put her feet on the desk while she made notes. The author, whoever he or she was, was very insightful. Emma flicked through the pages. She reflected on her own relationship with Alana and realized ruefully that she didn't know anything about bringing up a teenager. No, in answer to the author's question, she *didn't* know what made them tick. Were they really an unexploded time bomb, like Dr. Teen-Expert was suggesting? Emma took a quick glance at the dust cover, and then took a longer, keener look. Dr. Gray looked like he belonged on the cover of a men's fashion magazine. He was what her mother liked to call a "man's man": broad shouldered, with chiselled features and deep-set eyes. *I wonder what color they are*, Emma mused.

There was a knock at the door.

"Excuse me, I'm looking for –" a voice started. It was deep, with a pleasant timbre.

"You," Emma pointed.

"Me?"

"You're ... him," Emma added another word.

"Yes, I'm me," the speaker said with a smile full of patience.

In a burst of excitement, Emma's arms flailed like a baby chick leaving the nest on its maiden voyage ... and plunged headfirst in a backward-somersault onto the floor. The tall stranger rushed to help Emma untangle her legs from the office chair. The book landed spreadeagled beside her, the author's photograph in plain sight. *The black-and-white headshot does not do him justice*, Emma thought as she gazed at the real thing.

"You." She was back to one word again, this time pointing at the book.

The look of bemusement turned into a slight grimace, which was interrupted by the Police Boys' Club administrator who appeared at the door. "Sorry, Doctor, he's not here at the moment – sabbatical," she said by way of explanation. The woman looked down curiously at Emma, whose sprawled figure looked like an advertisement for *Don't Do Drugs*. "I see you've met Emma Oakley. She's looking after the Second-Chancers while he's away."

"Oh," the tall stranger said, taken aback. "I thought she *was* a Second-Chancer."

"You look better in color," Emma said.

He laughed and helped Emma to her feet. She stood woozily.

"I think you've taken quite a knock to the head," he said, concerned.

A high-pitched squawking from the phone

on the desk broke Emma from her trance. Her mother! She'd forgotten. She picked it up and held it like a microphone, enunciating each word into the mouthpiece, "I don't want to go out with a dentist." There was a second burst of sound, louder than the first.

The man, still holding Emma steady by the arm, looked amused. "Would you like to go out with *me*?" he challenged.

CHAPTER 9

A case of indigestion

Alana dashed to food technology after Elite Squad training, with her hair and clothes in complete disarray. Coach Kusmuk had taken great delight in pushing Alana beyond her physical limits, and could be heard snickering as she stumbled through the obstacle course *blindfolded* – a feat she hadn't made anyone else do. Despite being late, Alana took the time to give the lecture theater doors a quick spray from her mini bottle of lubricating oil – Alana packed with a Girl Scouts' thoroughness – for the hinges were notoriously noisy. Alana had no desire to make an embarrassing entrance during the celebrity chef's demonstration. Gibson High often invited experts to conduct workshops or to teach. It was considered a coup for the school, therefore, when TV Personality and Chef Extraordinaire, Isabella Thornton, agreed to visit to demonstrate her "Delectable Desserts."

"Just look at how the velvetiness of the butter and sugar combine to create a luscious, smooth, flowing caramel —" the chef's muffled voice could be heard through the widening crack. With one eye closed in concentration, Alana pushed the door an inch further. Isabella Thornton had thick, wavy, titian hair and skin the color of clotted cream. Her hourglass figure moved with grace as she navigated her way around the workspace. The smell which curled past Alana's nose reminded her of the local patisserie, which sold all her favorite desserts: chocolate éclairs, choux creams, and toffee pudding. It made her mouth water.

Isabella Thornton's voice was as silken and sweet as the ingredients she worked with. "There is something deliciously wicked about mingling the gooey syrupiness of this silky sauce with the tartness of these nubbly berries, which I'm going to let cascade through my fingertips, because really," she confided to the watching students from beneath long lashes, "nothing beats the feeling of plump, tumbling Forbidden Fruit." Vivid dots of color fell through her hands, each landing with a satisfying *plip* in the pile of stickiness. Through the wider crack of the door, Alana saw a sea of enthralled faces. Everyone sat mesmerized by the self-proclaimed Domestic Goddess, their eyes soft and unfocused. Alana knew they would never look at food the same way again. Her own eyes continued down the line. Khalilah's mouth hung wide open. Chef Thornton proceeded to "dollop sublime spoonfuls of ivory cream" onto the finished dessert. She dipped a delicate pinkie into the confection for a quick final taste. At the same time, Khalilah absentmindedly wiped a thin stream of drool from her chin. Khalilah never knew food could be so "naughty," "nubbly," and "sublime."

Alana squeezed her body through the now half-open door. Her stealthy entrance would have succeeded had Flynn not chosen this very moment to surprise her from behind. "Busted!"

he murmured, with a sharp prod in her back.

Clang! went the canister of oil onto the floor. Alana turned around to scold him, but was shocked into silence by his appearance. The scruff she was used to had disappeared. Flynn's shirt was tucked in, his hair was combed, and his shoes shone. The only nod to his former self was a tie which sat slightly loose at the neck, but it only added to his look of casual chic. He even smelled nice! Alana realized with shame that it was *she* who was the sweaty one, yet both of them were on Elite Squad. Obviously, while she'd been working on a covert entry, he'd spent that time "tidying up" for the special guest.

Flynn stepped forward, full of apologies. "*Bonjour! Mes excuses pour être en retard,*" he said to the astonishment of everyone, not least Alana, whose eyes had fallen out of their sockets. "*Comment magnifique!*" he exclaimed. "*Le muffin aussi ...*" he added cheekily.

Alana's eyes narrowed with fury. Alana didn't need much French to know that Flynn had just smooth-talked his way into the chef's good graces. She puffed up like a soufflé, stammering and suddenly breathless. Isabella Thornton smoothed wayward wisps of hair back with trembling fingers, leaving white, floury traces while she giggled into her hand. Flynn's distraction gave Alana time to gather her fallen belongings and slip into a chair without further trouble. Instead of feeling grateful, she felt absurdly mad.

Perhaps it was this pent-up rage which caused Alana's own muffins to emerge from the oven an hour later, blackened and rock-hard. Chef Thornton looked at her attempt with a pitying smile, prodding the unyielding lumps with a delicately painted fingernail. Miller's muffins were just as bad. He'd overdone the food coloring, as evidenced by the garish green of his hands, which he hid behind his back. Isabella Thornton sighed and made a point of avoiding the alien-looking blobs in their warm tray. When she reached Flynn's table, she merely collapsed into a heap of girlish giggles, batted her eyes, and left. Flynn turned and gave Alana an outrageous wink.

Alana felt the familiar *buzz* of the phone, set on silent, vibrate in her pocket. She had a message. She took advantage of the rowdiness in the classroom to check who it was from. James! The picture was of a fluffy kitten tussling with an oversized ball: *Soccer practice this weekend?* James had typed. The photo lifted her mood. She took a quick snap of her burnt muffins with the tag: *Gr8. I'll bring the snax.* In reply he sent a photo of a sumo wrestler's belly: *Cheers, but I already ate.*

Chef Thornton's announcement carried over the hubbub of excited voices. "Time for a taste-test, everybody. I'm very excited to see how you've all done. The baker of the plate voted most delicious will get a signed copy of my new book, *Bliss!*, and a private, one-on-one lesson with *moi*," she giggled, shooting a glance in Flynn's direction, "on exciting, exotic spices."

"Can I do anything to help?" Flynn offered as the chef took a second tray of her own muffins from the oven.

"Why, thank you. If you put them in that basket over there, I'll bring them to the staff room later."

Alana watched Flynn furtively empty *his own baking tray of muffins* into the Staff Basket, and the visiting chef's onto a plate marked "Number Nine" – labeled anonymously in the interests of objectivity and fairness. Flynn was cheating! But before Alana could say anything, Chef Thornton was urging them to eat the samples and vote for their favorite.

It was no surprise that Plate Number Nine attracted the most attention. When Maddie put the tiny wedge of muffin into her mouth, her eyes closed in ecstasy. She chewed slowly, savoring every bite. When she finally opened her eyes, her wide smile resembled a contented cat's. Intrigued by her friend's reaction, Sofia followed suit. Although her father, a successful restaurateur, produced delectable family meals on a nightly basis, Number Nine's muffin was just too delicious for words. "*Mmmm*," Sofia moaned, cheeks bulging. "You have *got* to try this," she urged Alana. "It is *so* unbelievably ..."

"– good. Yeah, I know."

"But how can you know if you haven't tried it?"

"Gut feeling," Alana said. *Like indigestion*, she thought.

Khalilah took her time sampling each plate. She was even brave enough to try Miller's green creations, although she soon regretted doing so. When Khalilah tried the muffin from the now-infamous Plate Number Nine, her eyes rolled back as she took a deep breath, and sighed. It really *was* sublime.

"Uh-uh-uh!" Isabella Thornton wagged a warning finger at one of the students, who was attempting to sneak a second serving from the plate.

Nobody was surprised when the muffin-maker of the most popular plate was declared the winner. "Congratulations, the owner of Plate Number Nine is Flynn Tucker!" Chef Thornton announced triumphantly.

"He can cook, too?" Khalilah exclaimed, with a catch in her throat.

For Alana, it was the last straw. There was a lot more to Flynn Tucker than met the eye, and she was determined to find it *all* out.

CHAPTER 10

Flynn the Phony

Alana thought she was pretty good at tailing people. She had some experience, after all, from following two suspects in last year's Case of the Missing Charm, when Sofia's charm bracelet had disappeared. On that occasion, she'd discovered the identity of the thief after investigating, sleuthing, and staking out behind pot plants which turned out to be too short. Then, with the help of her friends, she had laid some traps. She was sure she could find out more about the mysterious Flynn. She just needed the opportunity to follow him around.

Alana checked her notes on what she knew about him so far.

1. *Flynn can speak (some) French.*

2. *Flynn can play the saxophone well.*

3. *Flynn doesn't do any homework ... unless it's history.*

4. Flynn likes the TV program "Speedsters."

5. Flynn is a cheat and a liar.

6. Flynn does kickboxing, which only the Troubled Teens are allowed to do.

Alana drew an arrow between the last two points. Was there a connection? Was he part of the Troubled Teen program because of cheating or lying? Alana had to find out – if only to prove to her friends he really wasn't worth the amount of time they spent talking about him, which they'd taken to doing … a lot.

Alana had her chance the next day after school. Flynn was walking down King Street, Newtown, just around the corner from Gibson High. His school tie, which he'd taken off, made a slight bulge in his left pocket, and the top buttons of his shirt were undone. Without an audience, Alana noted, Flynn was back to his usual, slovenly self. King Street was not busy at this time of day, and it was difficult for Alana to follow him without being noticed, so she kept her distance and pretended to admire the art in shop windows. The exhibits were part of the Newtown Art Festival, and every year every shop participated, swapping their usual product displays for local paintings and sculptures.

There were some interesting pieces, some beautiful ones, and others just plain odd, but Alana barely noticed as she stood before the work titled "Flying Ducks" – a ceramic wall-hanging by Denise Nolan of three ducks, in graduating size, flying in the same direction. As it flew, the smallest duck covered its eyes, the medium-sized duck covered its ears, and the largest duck covered its beak. If Alana had been paying attention, she would have appreciated the humor of the See-No-Evil-Hear-No-Evil-Speak-No-Evil-birds, but she took them in with unseeing eyes, noting instead that Flynn had stepped into a gift shop selling novelty goods. "Probably stocking up on fart bombs and whoopee cushions," she grumbled to herself. He left ten minutes later. Empty-handed, Alana noted.

His next stop was a book store. Alana paused

before entering, again feigning an interest in the shop's window art. This time it was "Flying Decks" by the same artist. Three deckchairs, from small to large, flew with tiny wings that looked impossibly undersized for the weight they carried. Alana slipped in and gave the bookshelves a quick glance before choosing a spot far enough away from Flynn so he couldn't see her, but close enough so she could see what kind of books he liked. "Hmmm, so you're into Japanese *manga*, huh?" Alana muttered, writing this second observation down.

When Alana next looked up, Flynn was gone. Somehow he had slipped past her. She left the shop quickly and looked up and down the street. At first she didn't see him. All she could see were the usual hippy pedestrians, bodybuilders, and Goths wandering in and out of shops and cafés, but then she spied his lanky frame fifty meters away. Hands in pockets, slouched, school backpack flung casually over one shoulder. Alana hurried to catch up, and did so just before he strolled into his third store, a button shop. *A button shop?* Alana gazed after him in surprise but didn't dare get closer. The button shop sold only buttons. Hundreds of them. In all shapes and colors. But for all its variety, it was very small and impossible to hide in without being seen, so Alana looked at more window art. It was "Flying Docs" this time – same artist. Three doctors from the sci-fi TV series, *Doctor Who*, headed west looking almost puppet-like, with their extra-large heads and angelic wings. On this occasion Alana took the time to laugh.

When Flynn stepped out (again empty-handed) Alana was prepared. She hid by facing the other way, patting a silky terrier tied to a post. She counted to five slowly before glancing over her shoulder. If he was there, she could always pretend it was a coincidence and use the dog as an excuse. But Flynn was not there. He was crossing the road, making his way swiftly toward the florist, looking neither left nor right. Not that it would have mattered. Alana was careful to keep her back to him as he made his way back up the street. She gave the dog's soft coat one final stroke before following.

It was almost March. Summer was ending, and the flowers on display reflected the change of season. Alana liked flowers, especially gerberas for their bright reds, oranges, and yellows. They always looked so *happy*. She made a mental note to come back and take photos of them another time. James had taught her some new techniques using a macro lens, and she had yet to try them out.

"Why are you following me?" a voice said suddenly from behind.

Alana gave a start of surprise, turned and stared at Flynn. "Following you? I'm not following you! Who says I'm following you? That's ridiculous. I'm just looking at the art," she blustered.

Flynn didn't look convinced. "So you like Nolan's work, then?"

Alana looked at the display. "Denise Nolan," the card said in neat writing. She read the title of the work aloud. "'Flying Dacks.' Oh yes. Big fan. *Huge* fan of Nolan's work," she said, her confusion obvious.

"Hmmm. That's interesting. Very interesting," Flynn said thoughtfully. Against her will, Alana's gaze was dragged back to the work of the artist she was supposed to be an admirer of. Three pairs of men's full-brief underwear hung in the window. The kind her *grandfather* wore. One small. One medium. And one large. With wings. *Flying dacks.* Alana could feel herself blushing to the roots of her hair, and hurriedly averted her gaze. "It's funny, you know. I wouldn't have guessed you to be into Nolan's sculptures." Flynn's eyes, which were now the color of warm, flecked marble, sparkled with mischief. "But then they *do* say it's always the quiet ones you have to look out for. *Au revoir!* See you round school," Flynn said as he gave a wink and a little nod, and walked away. Before he had gone too far though, he called out, "And next time you follow me and don't want me to notice, you might want to change your hat."

Alana pushed back her mom's Mexican *sombrero* from her head and yelled, "I AM NOT FOLLOWING YOU!" so loudly that several passersby turned to stare. Flynn merely shrugged. It was a shrug which said, "Yeah right. That's what all the girls who follow me say." It was a shrug which said, "*C'est la vie.* I get followed all the time." It was a shrug which left Alana fuming. *So much for sleuthing incognito!*

Alana read what she'd added about Flynn to her list.

7. *Flynn likes novelty gear, Japanese manga, and buttons.*

She crossed out "buttons," which was most likely to have been a red herring. She took great satisfaction in adding one more point.

8. *Flynn is arrogant and conceited.*

She underlined the sentence three times, and wrote so hard that the tip of her pen made a hole through the paper.

Alana wandered back up King Street, still

fuming, until she reached the futon shop where she'd parked her bike. A small crowd stood in front of the window's display. Many of them were pointing and laughing.

"Not more Nolan art!" Alana grumbled, wondering what it could be this time. She ran through the alphabetical options and winced. Alana glanced across and saw a large sign which read "Sleeping Beauty" in curly, intricate writing. But it was what was beyond the sign which caught Alana's attention and made her catch her breath in surprise.

What was her mom up to now?

...

Rehabilitating the "Second-Chancers" was much harder than Emma thought it would be. So far they'd touched on the subject of "Job Seeking," which had revealed the urgent need for "Communication Skills." While this was a work in progress (and would continue to be throughout their lives, she imagined) Emma had turned her attention to "Team Building" on Dr. Gray's advice. He suggested that working together on a project that used their unique skills would boost their self-esteem.

But all the extra work had taken its toll, and Emma was physically and emotionally exhausted. The upcoming "date" with Dr. Gray added more weight on her shoulders. She hadn't had a "date" date in years. The need for respite led her to King Street, with all its delicious distractions: vintage shops, curios, quirky fashion, coffee, and sweet delicacies from the four corners of the globe. Emma stopped outside the futon shop and peered in. The artwork, "Sleeping Beauty," looked so tranquil, and the beds inside so inviting, she couldn't resist taking a peek. On impulse, she decided to enter. After all, she *could* do with a new daybed in her office. Noodle-the-Penguin had left too many souvenirs that couldn't be got rid of without industrial-strength bleach.

Emma tried the first futon. It was large and firm

and was said to be good for backs. "Too hard," she decided.

Emma tried the second futon. It was not as large and very squishy, perfect for snuggling, according to the sign. "Too soft," she said.

Emma tried the third futon. It was the same size as her daybed at home and gave slightly when she pushed on its surface. "Ahh, just right," she sighed. Her eyes closed, she adjusted her weight, shimmied into a comfortable position and … with the help of the painkiller she had swallowed for her toothache, fell asleep.

Although three bears *should* have come in at this point and pointed at Emma, shrieking, "There she is!" this is not what happened. Instead, Alana turned to the shopkeeper, whose bald head was as shiny as a bowling ball.

"Do you deliver?" she asked.

CHAPTER 11

Lost in translation

The first few classes of Mandarin covered the language's four tones and basic vocabulary. Alana was amazed by the sing-song cadences, which had syllables sliding down slippery dips, bouncing on trampolines, ascending to the sky and hovering in the air. Say "*ma*" using the wrong tone and you could be calling your mother a horse instead! Alana's partner for conversational Chinese was Miller. Miller never volunteered an answer and, if he was called upon to contribute, he mumbled or stared into space. Miss Wu reacted, first with patience, anger, and then she gave up. Miller, to all intents and purposes, was like wallpaper – there, but not really noticeable.

Jing Ren's and Jaey's presentation on introductions was Alana's first warning that something might be wrong.

"Nǐ hǎo. Wǒ de míngzì shì Jing Ren. Nǐ jiào

shénme míngzì?" Jing Ren said with confidence. (Hi. My name is Jing Ren. What's your name?)

Jaey replied, "Nǐ hǎo, Jing Ren. Wǒ de míngzì shì Jaey. Hěn gāoxìng jiàn dào nǐ." (Hi, Jing Ren. My name is Jaey. Nice to meet you.)

"Wǒ láizì Mǎláixīyà. Nǐ cóng nǎlǐ lái?" Jing Ren responded. (I'm from Malaysia. Where are you from?)

"Wǒ láizì Mǎláixīyà shì yě." Jaey said with a smile. (I'm from Malaysia, also.)

"Nà hěn bàng! Wǒ zài jiē lìng yīgè Mǎláixīyà de péngyǒu hē kāfēi. Nǐ xiǎng jiārù wǒmen ma?" Jing Ren said, struggling slightly with the long sentence. (That's great! I'm meeting another Malaysian friend for coffee. Would you like to join us?)

"Xièxiè. Wǒ xiǎng jiārù nǐmen." Jaey said with another grin. (Thank you. I would like to join you.)

Alana glanced at her notes, which looked and sounded vastly different. The class had been asked to come up with their own translations for a script based on the common theme "an invitation," so everybody's *would* be different, she reasoned.

She tried to ignore the alarm bells ringing in her brain. She had been assisted by Ling Ling, and surely she would know her Mother Tongue. Casting her mind back to Ling Ling's animated demonstration of the script, Alana mentally rehearsed all the tips she had been shown. According to Ling Ling, the four distinct tones of the language were just the beginning. There was flouncing, batting of the eyes, and hip-holding, too. "Like the French feminine and masculine, but more overt?" Alana had enquired. Ling Ling's answering cough could have meant anything.

Jing Ren and Jaey sat down while the class clapped politely.

"Alana and Miller," Miss Wu announced. The Mandarin teacher sat ramrod straight. Her face was as round as a peach and her skin flawless. She had the kind of hair used for shampoo commercials – silky, straight, and long – that hung to her waist. She nodded her head at Alana like a Chinese empress consenting for court to proceed.

"Nǐ hǎo, Alana," said Miller. (Hi, Alana.)

Alana replied, "Leiho bo?" with a friendly wave. (How are you doing?)

Miss Wu winced.

"Wǒ hěn hǎo, nǐ ne?" Miller mumbled. (I'm fine, and you?)

"Okay, loh." Alana remembered to push Miller playfully on the shoulder. "Wah seh, you so stylo milo today. You got pak toh izzit? (I'm okay. Wow, you look very stylish/fashionable today. Have you got a date?) Alana flicked her hair, batted her eyes, and put her hands on her hips.

Miller, taken aback by this sudden show of femininity, stuttered a thank-you. "Xièxiè."

Alana ignored the sound of Miss Wu's teeth snapping together and ploughed on. "Who izzit? Who izzit? I know her one, or not?" (Who is it? Who is it? Do I know her?)

Miller, unsure of what Alana was talking about, continued blindly.

Miller: "Wǒmen yìqǐ chī wǔfàn.""(Let's have

lunch.)

Alana: "Can ... can. Tài hǎo leh ... you belanjar?" (Sure, we can do that. Great ... your treat, right?) Ling Ling had been most emphatic about including this. Never go out, she warned, without deciding who was picking up the tab. When Alana protested, saying it sounded rude, Ling Ling had pushed her objections off the cliff.

Miller was relieved that their presentation was over. "Hǎo ba, wǒmen zǒu ba." (Okay, let's go.)

Alana turned to see the Mandarin teacher's face, no longer a subtle peach, more a livid beetroot. "What are you speaking?" Miss Wu asked, appalled.

"Umm, modern Mandarin?" Alana replied uncertainly.

"No, no, no. This is not Mandarin. This is an abomination!"

Alana's original hunch had been correct. She should *never* have taken up the offer from her mad-cap "aunt." But Auntie Ling Ling later defended her decision to teach Alana "Singlish" –

Singapore English – on social grounds. Singlish, she explained, was extremely useful when you wanted to hang out with friends, go shopping, or order food. It was a fusion of English, all four Chinese languages (Hokkien, Cantonese, Mandarin, and Teochew), Malay, and even Punjabi, reflecting the diverse, colorful blend of cultures living there. "Wah seh, how you expect to pick up boys with: 'Hi. My name is Alana. What's your name'? I mean, like, bo-ring!" she fake-yawned. "So obiang! Old fashion, lah, all that formal Mandarin."

"I'm not supposed to be picking up boys!" Alana fumed.

"Eh, I'm trying to make education more exciting, okay?" huffed Ling Ling, who slipped into more slang on the rare occasions she got angry. "And *practical*." She aimed a pointed look at Emma, who shrugged. "An zhua? (What's your problem?) You yaya papaya (arrogant) orreadly, (already) lah. Now you know more than me, dowan (don't want) my help. But I tell you," Ling

Ling wagged a warning fingernail of shimmering bronze, "learn proper way, where got fun one? Soo stoopid, you kuku-bird!" She grumbled under her breath. Ling Ling, her Singlish, and her pick-up lines disappeared in a blur of shimmery chiffon.

The next morning it was doubly frustrating when the school administrator did not transfer Alana to Malay as soon as she put in the request.

"Please, please, please," she begged, "I *have* to do Malay." She searched for a valid excuse and found nothing. "I'm desperate."

Mrs. Machlin shook her head. "That's not a good enough reason, Alana."

"Well no, I know, but ... I really, really, really have to transfer!" she insisted, lowering her voice. Her eyes skittered. She had just noticed someone else in the office.

Mrs. Machlin caught the panicked glance Alana shot Flynn and instantly drew the wrong conclusion. "I ... see. Desperate to 'learn Malay,' huh?"

"I'm not ... it's not because of ..." Alana

protested, but this only confirmed Mrs. Machlin's suspicions.

"It's alright, Sweetie," she whispered loudly. "I used to have a crush on Johnny Pike. He was as cute as a button. A bit of a 'bad boy' too," she added. Alana wanted to D-I-E! "Lucky for you it's the beginning of the term. Here," Mrs. Machlin said, handing Alana a piece of paper, "this is your amended timetable. Good luck with Malay!" she said with an exaggerated wink.

Alana left before Mrs. Machlin could do or say anything more to embarrass her. But she did risk one last look over her shoulder and caught Flynn's eye. His waggling eyebrows said it all. Naturally, after yesterday, Flynn would assume she was "desperate" to transfer to his class because of *him*. Alana left the office seething.

CHAPTER 12

Dating for Dummies

Alana knew her mom had a soft spot for animals, but even she was amazed when Emma, with a screech, stopped her from squashing a cockroach.

"Watch out! That's Harry!"

"Harry?" Alana repeated, confused.

"Or it could be Leo. It's hard to tell."

Harry-or-Leo showed no sign that he was facing death. In fact he showed no fear at all. If Alana didn't know better, it looked like the insect was waving his antennae in a gesture of welcome, in a "Hey, whassup? Make yourself at home" -kind of way. Any minute now he would offer them a beverage and light a cigarette. After all, if predictions about who would survive the end of the world were to be believed, this was *his* house, *his* world ... humans were merely temporary tenants. Alana shooed the bug away. It moved off with a reluctant scrabble.

"You're feeding it?" she accused her mom, holding a container of organic waste at eye-level, twisting it round and round. Mushy leaves of week-old spinach melded with apple cores, potato peelings, soggy beetroot, and limp carrots. Rude protrusions grew from knobby vegetable cuts as they squatted in the putrefying mass.

"Not really," Emma said, looking momentarily guilty before becoming distracted again.

"You know, if you don't put food scraps in the compost, they turn into a biohazard," Alana told her mom, whose sole response was a vague, "Uh huh."

"And gkjkdgj."

"Yes."

"And did you know sfhnaorfkh?"

"Really?"

"I knew it! You're doing it again, Mom. You're not listening!" Alana glared at her mother, who was still in her nightie, hair unbrushed, searching frantically under furniture on her hands and knees. Alana tamed her hair with a combination of sheer willpower and extra-strong gel, while Emma – like the strays she used to save – allowed hers to grow wild and roam free.

"Of course I listen, Clever Clogs. I've just got this awful deadline and I can't remember where I put my writing," Emma said, checking under the toaster and behind a potted plant for a missing piece of paper. Alana's mom, as a freelance journalist, got to do really amazing things sometimes, like interview rock stars like Slam Guru and people like Cristina Ibrahmovic, who had brought gymnastics to underprivileged children. But when she wrote up these interviews, she usually did them on whatever was handiest: paper napkins, telephone bills, even cereal boxes. The 1930s semi-detached terrace which Emma and Alana called home was long, narrow, and dark, which made it even more difficult to find the random pieces of paper upon which Emma wrote her ideas.

"She's feeding it!" Alana said to no one in particular. If she was honest, these expostulations were directed at her dad, for only Hugo would believe that Emma was nurturing cockroaches or had misplaced her writing. *Again.* Only he would understand Alana's frustration. Alana had an important soccer match coming up, class tests, now TWO torture-obsessed teachers, and Flynn-the-Fraud who her friends couldn't stop talking about. And if all that wasn't enough to cope with, home-grown toxic waste as well! "Worry-wart," she heard him chuckle in her head. "Oh, yeah?" she responded. "And I bet my birthday (horror of inevitable horrors) is going to be another Big Fiasco." "Big Heart," Hugo reminded her. If she concentrated *really* hard, she could almost feel him give a playful yank on her hair.

"*Ah ha!*" Emma exclaimed happily. "Microwave! It got wet. I had to dry it and …" she opened the door and retrieved a scrap of paper covered in blurry ink, "…*da dah!*" This time, it was a junk mail envelope. "Yes! Here it is!" She waved it in triumph. "Oww!" she said suddenly, clutching her jaw.

"What's wrong?"

"Oh, nothing. Just this stupid tooth again."

"You said you were fixing that tooth," said Alana, shouldering her school backpack. "You did make another appointment, didn't you?" Alana's eyes narrowed.

A second look of guilt flashed across Emma's features. How could she tell Alana that instead of seeing the dentist she was going on a date? She hoped these new painkillers did the trick ... she was beginning to think she needed something stronger. "Yes well, about that," she began, but was prevented from explaining further with the arrival of Katriona and Ling Ling.

Katriona strolled past the laundry basket and picked up a random pair of underwear. She eyed them with disgust, even though they were clean. They were, she decided, a metaphor for her friend's life: over-stretched, bedraggled, and outdated. She dangled them on a long finger with a grimace.

"We need to go shopping."

"Oh, not again," Alana moaned. The purchases her mom made in the company of her friends were never very practical. Katriona and Ling Ling were responsible for the Mexican *sombrero* Alana had used to "hide" from Flynn. The hat had failed as a fashion statement and been equally disastrous as camouflage. Chastened, it sat on the kitchen bench cradling a watermelon.

"Don't worry, Alana," Katriona smirked, "I'm sure we can find *you* a nice little pair. I saw some Little Bo Peep ones the other day."

Alana gave a sugar-coated smile of steel. "No thanks. But," she looked up and peered closely at Katriona's face, so close she could see the hair in Katriona's greyhound-thin nostrils, "Auntie Katriona, you might want some anti-aging cream for yourself. Aren't those *crow's feet* on your face?" Alana asked, her tongue hijacked by a whim of devilry.

Katriona looked horror-struck as she rushed to find a mirror. Alana was reminded of Edvard Munch's painting, *The Scream.* She wondered if Munch had played a similar joke and told his model, "You've got wrinkles," and then said,

"Hold that pose."

Ling Ling noticed the tub of organic waste still in Alana's hand. "Eww, what's *that*?" she asked.

"It's for the compost," Emma explained. "It makes great fertilizer. Some people even use raw vegetables on their skin." Emma was an avid reader of all topics and, like Sofia and Mr. Hornby the math teacher, collected trivia with the same fervor she had for collecting strays.

Katriona rushed back into the kitchen. "What for?" she cried. Neither Katriona nor Ling Ling ate many vegetables, and when they did it was usually by mistake. That vegetables could be of benefit to the skin *from the outside* was news to them.

"It has rejuvenative qualities," Emma explained.

"So people shove gunk like that on their face to help them look younger?" Katriona asked with urgency.

"Well," Emma said uncertainly, "kind of."

"Great. We'll take it," and with all thoughts of underwear shopping banished from her mind, Katriona snatched the container of rotting vegetation from Alana and clomped to the door as fast as her five-inch wedges allowed. The idea of fruity face masks and vegetable facial scrubs required further investigation. Immediately!

Ling Ling gave an apologetic shrug and turned to go – but not before slipping a DVD called *Dating Simulation* into Emma's hand with a wink.

Emma was careful to conceal the newly acquired DVD behind her back as she kissed "LaLa" goodbye. Alana had many names. She was Clever Clogs, or Darling Girl, or LaLa to her mom, and sometimes Lani or Lana-Iguana to her friends. Katriona secretly called her Piranha – Alana Piranha – because, to Katriona, the name suited her to perfection: a small, ferocious beast with sharp teeth that tore you apart and asked questions later. With that kind of reputation, Emma was reluctant to tell Alana anything about her upcoming date with Dr. Gray.

When Emma finally had the house to herself, she slipped the DVD into the player and pressed "Play." The head and shoulders of a handsome

Japanese man appeared on the screen. He smiled. He nodded. His facial expressions changed from one of sympathy to polite humor. Suddenly, he laughed out loud. It was all very baffling. The instructions were little help: *No lonely anymore! They promised. Date-boy be your friend. Smile. Have fun. Say, Cheese!* With a start, Emma realized she was expected to practice "conversing" with the screen "date," who made sympathetic noises and sounds.

"Hi, my name is Emma," she began. "No. Scrap that. You know my name already. Umm, I really enjoyed your book."

The Japanese man gave a slight smile and shrug. *Wow*, Emma thought. *Not a bad start.*

"Have you always liked working with teenagers?"

The man's face broke into an enthusiastic grin. Emma was amazed: *I'm really good at this!*

"I'm feeling pretty nervous."

The man smiled in sympathy. *I'm on a roll!* She chortled.

Hours later, Katriona and Ling Ling returned.

Emma was still in her nightie with her hair unbrushed. The skin of Katriona's face was a lurid green, while Ling Ling's was a blotchy, bright purple.

"Look at this, look at this," Emma cried, her mouth overflowing with popcorn. She turned to the man on the TV screen. "My feet stink so bad, people usually ask me what died!"

On cue, the Japanese "date" threw his head back and gave a throaty chuckle.

"I'm on fire!" Emma said excitedly.

Katriona ripped the snack bowl from Emma's unresisting fingers and bent down until they were eye-to-eye. "You. Are. Not. Taking. This. Seriously. Enough," she bit out.

Emma drew back suddenly from the green ghoul who had replaced her friend. "What happened to your face?" she said, aghast.

"You!" her friends howled with such Wicked-Witch-Of-The-East-like fury that Emma wished she had magical ruby slippers to click together to escape home. Not that it would have helped, she remembered ...

She *was* home!

CHAPTER 13

One step forward, two steps back

Saturday night arrived all too soon for Emma who – after a week of anxious waiting – was a bundle of nerves. Katriona and Ling Ling solved the problem of how to tell Alana by turning up with an armful of clothes and makeup for Mom's Hot Date. Alana was fine once she'd established the Hot Date was over 18. She did *not* want a repeat of the Jet Tierbert fiasco!

"Grandma will be happy," was all she said.

Emma wasn't too pleased to be reminded of that fact, but she was very pleased with her appearance. Katriona and Ling Ling had worked their Makeover Magic. Gone was the soft, tatty, comfortable nightie. Gone was the bushy, untameable mane. Gone was the excessive hair that had invaded her eyebrows, underarms, and legs. In their place was a sleek, sophisticated woman ready for her first Real Date in seventeen years, with a man she met only a week ago, who looked like a male model …

Emma felt sick.

Five minutes later, Katriona and Ling Ling were pounding on the door of her office, where Emma huddled under the covers of her new futon. Her heart was racing and she was finding it hard to breathe. She looked around at her familiar surroundings and listed them in her head for comfort. Desk covered with reference books, papers, and last night's dishes. Okay, she conceded, last *week's* dishes. *Check.* Computer. *Check.* Extra-large, green Christmas tree, covered with ornaments, and random scraps of paper with ideas for articles. *Check.* Bookshelves with favorite novels, family photo albums, and more reference titles. *Check.* Essential oils air freshener for calm and relaxation. *Check.* (She took a quick sniff. No change. Darn.) Claypot. Never used. *Check.* Pressure cooker. Used once but stopped after it acted like a rocket. *Check.* Food processor. Not used after she almost lost a finger. *Check*. Her eyes continued their path around the room and settled on a book. *Teenage Terrorism* by Dr. Oliver Gray. Emma kicked it out of sight with a squeal.

"Emma, open the door!" Katriona yelled.

"I need to touch up your hair," Ling Ling cried.

Emma felt her hair. It was already starting to puff up.

"I know it's doing that poufy thing again," Ling Ling added.

"I'm not coming out," Emma yelled. "I'm not doing it. I can't do it. You can't make me!" she cried, smearing off the carefully applied lipstick, running frantic fingers through her hair, and slipping back into her tatty nightie with a mixture of relief and defiance.

The door reverberated as the pounding resumed with more urgency. It bounced on its hinges. *Thud. Thud. Thud.*

"Are you okay?" Emma heard a small voice at her elbow. It was Alana. Katriona and Ling Ling had forgotten about the second entrance to the room. Alana made her way toward her mom the same way a veterinarian approaches an injured animal. Emma, with her racoon eyes and a slash for a mouth, held out her arms. Alana dove into them and squeezed.

Thud. Thud. Thud.

Ping-pong pealed the doorbell.

Thudthudthudthudthudthud.

Emma and Alana looked at each other. Emma gave a tiny nod. Alana opened the office door. It was Katriona. Ling Ling was peering through the peephole of the front door.

"He's here," they heard Ling Ling cry.

Katriona's shocked gasp brought Ling Ling running into the office like a streak of sunshine.

"*Wah lao, eh!*" (Oh no!) she cried. "Why like that?"

Emma shook her head. "I can't do it. Tell him I'm sick. But not too sick," she said, biting her lip. "Nothing so contagious that he won't want to see me again." Ling Ling made to go. Emma grabbed at Ling Ling's arm. "But nothing I can recover from too quickly." Emma sagged like a sail that had lost its wind. "I'm just ... not ready."

The doorbell rang a second time.

Ling Ling wrenched her arm away and rushed to the front door. She put one curly, fake eyelash to the hole in the door. "Wah seh! So handsome, loh," she said, her voice heavy with disappointment.

"Really?" Katriona smoothed her hair. "How handsome?"

"Very, *very* handsome. Sayang," she muttered, staring at Emma darkly. "What a waste!" Just as quickly, Ling Ling calmed down as she took charge of the situation. She was a Shu, wasn't she? Hadn't her ancestors survived the Wall Street crash of 1929? She could do this.

"Aiyah, I will handle it." Ling Ling gave a quick spray of the essential oil (for calm and relaxation), behind her ears, under her arms, and a final squirt in her mouth for good measure. She opened the door wide, mouth pursed like a prune. "Hi hi! You must be Dr. Gray. Wah, you very stylo milo one!"

CHAPTER 14

Alana has a ball

Alana had been looking forward to Sunday soccer practice all week, particularly soccer practice with Uncle James. She had high hopes this year. Their five-a-side team promised to be really tight with the addition of Khalilah, who turned out to be a skilful goalie. Not much got past her and, if it did, it wasn't because she hadn't leapt into the air to a ridiculous height or thrust out a leg at an impossible angle. Khalilah was a vast improvement on Sofia, whose strategy was to close her eyes and point the Confuse and Defeat Your Enemies Magical Talisman at incoming balls. Sofia willingly gave up her position to play reserve. She was running out of amulets.

Sometimes the rest of the team joined Alana for soccer practice in one of the local parks. Sometimes it was just her and James. On this occasion everybody was there, and they practiced passing while they waited for him to turn up.

Apart from Sofia and Khalilah, the two other girls on their team were the Ashley twins, Prita and Preyasi. It was impossible to tell them apart. Both had dark brown hair and skin the color of strong tea. Both were petite and fast. They'd earned the nickname "Pocket Rockets," a far cry from the real meaning of their names, which was "Dear One" and "Beloved." They always wore the same outfits and often spoke at the same time. It was like listening in stereo. When they didn't speak together, they finished each other's sentences – a habit Alana found just as spooky. Their footwork was telepathic too, and they worked fluidly on the field.

Alana felt they had a good chance this year to chalk up some decent points, especially now they had the twins *and* Khalilah in goal. To date, the soccer competitions had been dominated by the Soccer Academy – students who had been training since before they could walk. Although Gibson High trained hard, they had never collected enough points to compete in the more serious leagues. It was critical they won the next game.

James arrived at the field soon after the girls began their two-kilometer warm-up.

"Ooh," said Maddie, "someone got into a fight with a lawnmower and lost," she teased.

James gave her a good-natured grin and fell into step next to them. He had no trouble matching the girls' pace. James's longish locks *had* been trimmed and he looked good, although they would never dare tell him that. His hair now just scraped the bottom of his nape, and in the heat, he had wrapped a bandana around it to keep it off his neck.

"A little less talk and a little more action, thanks," he said, picking up the pace.

"Oh yeah? Let's see how fast you can run then, old man," Prita and Preyasi both challenged. The two-kilometer jog turned into a two-kilometer sprint. Sofia was the first to drop away, and Khalilah soon joined her. By the end of it, Maddie and the twins were neck and neck, with James not far behind. Not bad, considering Alana had wrestled onto his back for a piggyback ride!

"No (*pant, pant*) fair," James gasped, falling to the ground. The girls giggled and ran to get the ball.

"Come on, Uncle James," Alana teased, "we're not going to win the next game by lazing around."

James jumped up to give her a tickle before leading them in some drills. By the time they were finished, everyone was hot and sweaty and in need of a cold drink. While the others scooted off to the Milk Bar across the road to grab one (and to chat about Flynn), Alana continued practicing with James, relishing the one-on-one time.

Alana and James began with headers. *Pum*, the ball went as it bounced off Alana's head into James' waiting hands. Before long they had worked themselves into an easy rhythm.

"Mom had a date last night," Alana said mid-bounce.

James fumbled the ball – it rolled away to the side. He walked over with slow, measured steps to retrieve it. He picked it up and resumed practice, saying casually, "Really? A *date*?"

Pum.

Alana wasn't fooled. "Yep. A doctor, too. Auntie Ling Ling thought he was very, very handsome, loh," she said in a perfect copy of Ling Ling's nasal tones.

"A doctor, huh?"

Pum.

"He's some teenage specialist author guy," she said, watching his face closely.

Pum.

"Well, *I've* tried knocking sense into you with this ball for years, but it hasn't done much good," he teased with another accurate aim at Alana's head. "Maybe your mom needs some expert advice," he said lightly. "How do *you* feel about it?"

Alana caught the ball and transferred it to her feet, bouncing it up and down from knee to toe in a trick James had taught her long ago. She shrugged. "I don't know," she said honestly. "It's good, I suppose. I want her to be happy ... and she has been in her own way. But I get the feeling now she needs more ..." she trailed off.

"And having a new guy in *your* life is okay?"

Alana's cheeks dimpled. "Well, of course he would have to pass my very stringent test first."

James motioned for Alana to pass the ball, and she did so. It now shuttled smoothly between their feet. "And that would be?" he asked.

"Uh, uh," she wagged a finger. "No cheating. I'm not giving any hints to the contestants. Although," she said with a sly look, "decent taste in music is an absolute must."

James gave a loud laugh. Alana's favorite band at the moment was a group of 20-somethings who called themselves *Dead Dogs Rotting*. Heavy on the electric guitar and even heavier on the drums, they had attracted hardcore fans like flies to their name. "So the golden oldies are out?" he asked with a cheeky grin.

"Absolutely."

"Easy listening music?"

Alana made a gagging noise.

"Disco?" he asked, eyebrows raised.

"Definitely not."

James gave a theatrical sigh. "Guess I'm out of the running, then."

"Alana!" It was Khalilah. "Are you coming?" she called out from across the field. It looked like she'd found a cream bun.

Alana gave Khalilah a thumbs-up sign and then grabbed the ball, hugging James with one arm. "Thanks," she said against his chest.

James hugged her back. "You're welcome."

"For practice too," she added as she let go.

James nodded gravely. "You're welcome."

As James headed off to his car, Alana called his name. He turned with a ready smile.

"She didn't do it, you know."

"*Who* didn't do *what*?"

"Mom. She didn't go through with the date. Said she couldn't."

James let that thought sink in before replying in an upbeat way, "Oh!"

Alana and her friends yelled their final thanks

and goodbyes to James from a distance. Alana's last image of James was of one hand raised in acknowledgement, the other in his pocket, and a thoughtful look on his face.

CHAPTER 15

"And though she be but little.
She be fierce ..." Shakespeare

It was now April, which meant "Shakespeare Week" for the Year Eights at Gibson High to celebrate the birth of William Shakespeare in 1564. A range of activities had been organized. Students were given the opportunity to learn Elizabethan dances, exchange insults in Shakespearean language, and listen to senior students performing the courtly music popular during Shakespeare's time.

Alana noticed that Miller and his friends, Colin Johnson and Chris Kruger, took particular delight in abusing each other in Shakespeare-speak every lunch hour as they played their favorite computer game.

"Methink'st thou art in need of a good kick up the buttocks, thou cankerous, beetle-headed dotard!" Miller yelled with glee.

"Oh yeah? Eat my knickers, oh beslubbering, swag-bellied canker-blossom!" Colin cried.

"My finger in thine eye, thou mammering, toad-spotted maggot-pie!" Chris responded as he punched frantically on the keyboard.

Colin Johnson was a stocky boy and one of the few in Year Eight with the beginnings of facial hair. A faint line of fuzz sat incongruously above his rosebud mouth. Colin's pale blonde hair was cut closely and evenly to his scalp. And he always had a pen or two tucked behind his ears. Their shell-like shape had changed permanently from the constant burden to resemble a launching pad. Mostly that's what people saw. Not his hazel green eyes but the top of Colin's head bent down in concentration as he drew. Colin was only ever comfortable with a pen or pencil in his hand ... or a joystick.

While Colin gave the impression of pale fuzz, Chris Kruger, was all hair. He had a dark curly mountain of it as well as a set of furry earmuffs over his ears, all year round. A pair of thick eyebrows sat like two caterpillars over Chris's dark deep-set eyes. Chris Kruger reminded Alana of a villain from the silent black and white films – hunched over with both hands rubbing together in fiendish pleasure.

Today, Chris was doing just that because the Year Eights were in the Newtown Theater to perform their favorite lines from Shakespeare's plays. Not only Chris was excited. The buzz of anticipation from all the Year Eights was tangible. There was some good-natured jostling as to who would go first.

"Your attention, please," their English and drama teacher called out. Dr. Olivier looked over his bright pink spectacles and glared a couple of talkers into silence before continuing. "The theater is warmer than we'd like because the air-conditioning is down, but I'd still like to see lots of movement, expression, and emotion. Remember to project your voice and to *feel* the words." Dr. Olivier liked to grab at the air when he said the word "feel" and he said the word "feel" a lot. Students were always being encouraged to "feel the words," or "feel the pain," or "feel the emotion," while he waved his arms like a conducting pelican.

Dr. Olivier consulted his clipboard. "Could we have Chris Kruger, Colin Johnson, and Miller White to the stage, please?"

The three boys were dressed in futuristic costumes and pushed a homemade robot onto the stage from the wings. It wasn't the chance to perform drama which had Chris excited but the opportunity to drive the mechanical contraption he had made. Chris – a self-confessed "petrol head" – manipulated the machine on the stage with difficulty, dressed as he was in his own robot costume. Chris wished he could keep working on it but he had to sneak the robot's motor back into his grandfather's electronic scooter before it was missed.

There was some giggling when the students noticed Colin wearing a dress and pink fluffy boots. It was interesting to note, however, that the boy's usually tremulous voice, which bordered on a stutter, disappeared while he performed. Swords clashed. Insults in Shakespeare-speak were exchanged. Spaghetti guts erupted from Miller's abdomen. It was hard to see what the boys' performance had to do with Shakespeare at all, but apparently evil aliens were fought and given the boot, quite literally, by a victorious Colin.

The three boys exited the stage – Miller-the-Alien limping – followed by the sound of tentative clapping. By the time they ran back to take a bow, all clapping had ceased.

"Awkward," Maddie whispered in a sing-song voice to Alana.

"Right, well, thank you boys. I think. I could really *feel* the urgency of that scene. Well done. Back to reality now, people. Let's have Flynn Tucker, shall we?" Dr. Olivier mopped his bald head, which had become slick with sweat, and sat down. "When you're ready, thanks, Flynn." The theater quietened.

In an instant Flynn was striding around the stage like a matador. Two hands shook out an imaginary cape and slowly curled up into twin fists over Flynn's mouth. His shoulders hunched forward. Everybody's eyes tracked the slightest movement he made. What would Flynn perform? Othello? Hamlet? Macbeth? Curiosity and anticipation had everyone leaning forward in their seats.

A curious sound emerged from Flynn's mouth. It sounded like spitting and coughing and a little bit like ... a ... train?

Was Flynn *beatboxing*???

I wrote **sonnets**,

I mean come on **man**,

I never **stumbled** or **mumbled**,

On my **magic** and I'll take it **backwards**,

After what **happened**,

When I was a boy I **backslapped**,

Yeah! **Backhanded.**

But the **fact** is…

I'm a legendary **poet**,

And everybody **knows** my name,

And I'm here to **show it**,

To **show** the way,

Don't believe me I'd be like **open sesame**.

I've got the keys now I'm out of this **cage**.

All the world's a **stage**,

And I'm a **main role**,

Performed a lot of masterpieces,

That they found **gold**,

My language is so **great that** it's in your **education**,

I had a disaster with my family,

It took **dedication**,

Look **straight man**,

I've finished **debating**,

I'm not gonna waste my time **reciting like crazy**,

I'm a **celebrity**,

Death is a **comedy**,

My plays are **comically funny**,

I mean **honestly**,

You can never **conquer me logically**,

I'm the **prophecy**,

The people can't get **enough of me**.

With a dramatic flourish, Flynn held out a skull. A skull that ordinarily would have prompted the "Alas, poor Yorick!" line from one of Shakepeare's plays, but instead became the prop for Flynn's finale ...

So this is I,

Yes this is **me**,

As you look yes as you look and **see**,

Call me an **MC**

Of the **15th century**

I am a **masterpiece**,

Like Midsummer Nights **Dreams**.

(Taken from *The Shakespeare Rap* by William Brien)

The Year Eight audience began whistling and clapping. Before Dr. Olivier could thank Flynn and compliment him on his innovative rap which *overflowed* with feeling, Sofia jumped up on stage, startling the skull from Flynn's hand. It dropped to the floor and rolled onto its side, sockets empty and mouth ajar in a hideous grin. "Doubt that the stars are fire, Doubt that the sun doth move his aides, Doubt truth to be a liar, But never doubt I love."

Alana smacked her hand on her forehead with a sharp *slap*. What was Sofia doing? Where was the girl's pride? Did she even know what she was saying? With one look at Sofia's face, Alana realized that she did. Alana ran up on stage with her costume – a donkey's head – tucked under her arm, and leapt between the two with a loud *thud*. "Love sought is good, but giv'n unsought is better," she appealed to Sofia, meaningfully jerking her head behind her at Flynn. But her friend was past caring.

"Can one desire too much of a good thing?" Sofia argued.

Much to the two girls' astonishment, Khalilah replied, joining them on stage. "We cannot fight for love, as men may do. We should be wooed and were not made to woo."

But Sofia, having taken the first step toward revealing her true feelings, wasn't giving up, especially with a romantic rival declaring her own interest. "*I'll* follow thee and make a heaven of hell, to die upon the hand I love so well," she implored a very confused Flynn.

Alana tried to inject some sense into her friends once more. "Expectation is the root of all heartache."

This time it was Maddie who chimed in as she too joined them. "The course of true love never did run smooth."

Flynn's attempt to speak was squashed by Alana, who pushed him away with one hand and warned him, "Give thy thoughts no tongue," then turned to her friends to plead, "Tis one thing to be tempted, another thing to fall!"

But Flynn was determined to have some say, even if he wasn't quite sure which Shakespeare play they were performing. "The lady doth protest too much, methinks."

Alana's lip curled. "Do you think I am easier to be played on than a pipe?"

Flynn answered with a smug shrug. "Suspicion always haunts the guilty mind."

"The empty vessel makes the loudest sound," she said, knocking on his head with exaggerated strokes. This brought an appreciative chuckle from the audience. Meanwhile, Dr. Olivier flicked through the papers of his clipboard to make sense of the performance. *First alien warfare, a rap, and now this?* He pulled at his collar and adjusted his bow tie. So far, the group had recited lines from at least five different Shakespeare plays!

The three girls pushed Alana out of the way and advanced.

"Hear my soul speak: The very instant that I saw you, did my heart fly to your service," Khalilah beseeched Flynn.

He took a step back.

"What made me love thee? Let that persuade thee," Sofia implored. "There's something extraordinary in thee. I cannot: but I love thee; none but thee; and thou deserves it."

Flynn stepped back again.

"Such is *my* love, to thee I so belong, That for thy right myself will bear all wrong," Maddie said passionately.

Flynn looked from the adoring girls to the audience. Grinning like a Cheshire cat, he gloated,

"I bear a charmed life," until he realized the trio had backed him into a corner. "Thou art very close," he yelped.

"Love is a smoke made with the fume of sighs," Alana muttered. "And yet, to say the truth, reason and love keep little company together nowadays." It was as if all of them had forgotten the audience and were reenacting Shakespeare's words for real. *Time to bring this "performance" to a close before they make even bigger fools of themselves*, Alana thought to herself. She thrust the donkey's head from *A Midsummer Night's Dream* onto Flynn's head and dragged him off stage. "That it should come to this!" she declared, throwing her hands in the air in disgust.

"Good night, good night! Parting is such sweet sorrow," called Khalilah, one hand outstretched. Her fingertips brushed the rough hairs of the donkey costume as Flynn was led away. The girls sighed, lost in their own world of Shakespearean tragedy.

"Indeed, a very courageous effort from you all,"

Dr. Olivier said, breaking into the girls' trance. "Thank you for that unique and ..." he cleared his throat, "*extraordinary* ... representation of Shakespeare's work. I don't think I've ever heard so many plays and sonnets performed all at once," he said, mopping his head profusely and wringing the material out. The audience erupted into applause. Shakespeare's words *had* come alive with real sincerity. And the rap in the beginning about William Shakespeare had been really amazing! The theater rang with cries of "Encore! Encore!" Alana led Flynn back on stage to join the girls, forcing the furry, unseeing head up and down to take a bow.

"Always knew you were a donkey brain," she whispered to Flynn.

Flynn gave a good-natured "*Hee-haw!*" and all five of them took another bow.

...

Sofia, Maddie, and Khalilah rushed up to Flynn as soon as it was time to return to Gibson High, leaving Alana to struggle with the unwieldy donkey costume.

"You were so great back there, Flynn-ster," Sofia said, looking at Flynn from beneath long eyelashes as she twisted the strands of purple hair around her fingers.

"Oh, thanks," Flynn replied.

"I thought you were amazing," Khalilah breathed, looking up at him adoringly.

"You guys were good too," he said.

Khalilah and Sofia giggled into their hands, just as Chef Thornton had done. But because Khalilah wasn't looking where she was going, she tripped over a bump in the pavement. Flynn stopped her from falling just in time. "Thanks, Flynnie," she breathed.

"'Flynnie'? That's a ridiculous name! He's not a baby," said Sofia.

"At least it's better than 'Flynn-ster.' 'Flynn-ster' ... it sounds like 'monster.'"

"If you think Flynn-ster is bad, wait til you hear what Maddie calls him ... 'Big F,'" Sofia scorned.

"You don't mind, do you, Big F?" Maddie said defensively.

But "Big F" had crept away from the bickering girls. Things were getting way too weird. Alana shook her head as she watched her three friends chase after Flynn with cries of, "Flynn-ster!" "Flynnie!" and "Big F!" Alana realized in horror that her friends were stuck – not in a love triangle, but a love square! The sooner she discovered the truth about "Flynn-the-Phony," the better.

...

Back at the school clinic, Nurse Cathy put down the electric drill and lifted her visor to stare at the headless skeleton hanging limply on its hook

... Drat! Someone had nicked the skull. How could she practice the bolotomy now? Or was it lobotomy? Medicine was so confusing. She looked around the room. Her gaze fell on both of her bandaged patients. Patient X managed to look panic-stricken.

The door swung open.

"Oh, Nurse Cathy! Thank goodness you're in. I have the most awful migraine," a voice croaked.

Nurse Cathy beamed as she ushered her new patient in. "I've got just the thing, Mrs. Snell," she said, revving the motor of her electric drill.

Some time later, Nurse Cathy looked in the mirror in consternation. How did the number eight come to be on her forehead? She peered closer. A definite imprint was there, like a stamp pounded into her skin. She looked down at her hand. And why was she holding these headache tablets? The last thing she remembered was searching for the skull of her skeleton. And then Mrs. Snell had come in... Nurse Cathy peered at the mirror again, realizing for the first time that the stamp looked a lot like the number eight on Mrs. Snell's knitting needle.

"She didn't... she wouldn't... nooooo..." Nurse Cathy dismissed the fanciful thought that the sweet, gummy, great-grandmotherly Mrs. Snell had anything to do with the mysterious mark.

Nurse Cathy rubbed her head. That number eight was *sore*!

Looking down at the headache tablets in her hand, she said, "Good thing I've got these!" congratulating herself on what a fine nurse she was.

CHAPTER 16

Detention in the dungeon

Alana hated to admit it, but she was stumped. It was mid-April and she was no closer to unraveling the mystery of Flynn-the-Phony. Such was his popularity amongst her friends that the three girls refused to hear a word against him. Maddie and Flynn met regularly online to jam together with other cyber-friends. He was teaching Sofia how to twirl her drumsticks, and she was teaching him how to read palms, and now and then he shared fudge brownies from the school bakery with Khalilah. *Probably stolen, Alana thought uncharitably as she kicked a wall.*

"Hi, Alana," Flynn would call out, but Alana never replied. She would rather cut out her tongue, skewer it, and feed it to an army of red ants before she spoke to that creep. "You could just give him a chance, you know," Maddie had said to Alana one day. But Alana wasn't interested in giving Flynn a chance and even less so when Sofia had suggested it had something to do with Hugo.

"You think I don't want to like Flynn because of my dad?" Alana had asked, alarmed.

"No, I'm saying that just because you like someone doesn't mean you're *betraying* your dad," Sofia struggled to explain.

"You think I want to *date* my dad?" Alana cried.

Sofia's dreads flew about her head in an emphatic blur. "No, of course not! I'm just saying that it's okay, you know. To like a boy. It doesn't mean you like your dad any less. In fact your dad would probably approve."

But on this Alana was adamant. "Not of Flynn, he wouldn't." She knew Flynn had something to hide and she was not giving up until she found out what.

At least the girls were no longer caught up in the trigonometry of unrequited love. They had come to their senses after realizing Flynn was interested in them as friends, and nothing more. Upon reflection, the girls felt embarrassed about the way they had behaved and blamed Tierbert-fever for their actions. NO ONE should ever come between them and their friendship, said Sofia. The others agreed.

"But if *Jet Tierbert* fell for me, sorry guys, but you'd be dropped faster than a pair of my brother's underwear," Sofia conceded, now that her brothers had taken to "mooning" Jehovah's Witnesses, census recorders, and any other unsuspecting visitors who came to call. It was so bad Sofia's mom had added the warning "and kids" to the "Beware of the Dog" sign which hung on their front gate.

"*He's such a gentleman*," Alana said, mimicking Khalilah. "Gentleman, my *derrière*," she grumbled.

"I hope you have a good explanation for defacing school property, Miss Oakley," a voice rang out.

Alana shook off the cloud of dark thoughts and looked at Coach Kusmuk. The petite figure had her arms crossed and was tapping a size-3 trainer. A pointed glance downwards made Alana look at the damage she'd caused: a neat, shoe-shaped hole that her football boot had hollowed out.

"This building is part of the National Trust. Do you know what that means? It means that it has a High Historical Value. And I, for one, do not appreciate you kicking it into rubble."

Crud!

"Ordinarily I'd suggest a grueling workout on The Scream, but you can have detention with Mrs. Snell instead," the P.E. teacher smirked.

"But I've got soccer practice," Alana wailed. "The big game is coming up."

"Too bad. You should have thought of that before waging war on unarmed bricks and mortar. You'd better hurry," she added with a glance at her watch which looked too heavy for her wrist, "I hear Mrs. Snell doesn't like students to be late."

Alana grabbed her school bag and kit and rushed off with an apologetic glance at Khalilah, who was putting on goalkeeper's gloves. "Where are you going, Alana? We've got training," she yelled.

Alana could only shrug as she jogged backwards. "Sorry. Got detention. I'll explain la-"

Alana sped down one flight of stairs. Then two. Three. The room reserved for detention was deep in the bedrock of the school's basement, and Alana noticed a sudden drop in temperature with each descending floor. The clock in the room read 3:04. She made it into her seat seconds before the bell sounded. Mrs. Snell snapped the door shut and gave the detainees a gruesome smile that looked far from friendly. Apart from Alana, there were Miller White and his sci-fi buddies, Chris Kruger and Colin Johnson, as well as a senior boy and girl.

"It's lovely to see you all. I do so enjoy this special bonding time we can share. Just us. Alone. In this soundproof room. With ALL my favorite toys, I mean, historical artifacts." Mrs. Snell paused to run an admiring finger along the torture devices displayed on the walls: heavy metallic objects with pointy spikes and ominous-looking chains. The air was cold and clammy. Alana shook off the feeling they were in a dungeon. "Do you hear that, children? That is Peace and Quiet. So soothing when you have a migraine. No noises of planes flying overhead. Or trains pounding underground. Just us and a little friend I like to call 'Silence.' Let's keep it that way, shall we?" And with a grin that displayed too many false teeth, Mrs. Snell waddled to her seat and sat down. They watched her put two mysterious pills in her mouth. With a toad-like swallow, they were gone.

Before long they could hear the familiar *creak, creak, creak* of the chair as the teacher rocked back and forth, the *click, clack* of her knitting needles, and the smacking of her dentures. Alana, who was good at noticing things, saw that the knitting project had overly long arms.

Like it was meant for an orangutan.

The students found it difficult to sit still. It wasn't long before Colin Johnson began to doodle, Chris Kruger found something to eat, and Miller White – next to Alana – began to read. The seniors were seated too far away to know what they were up to. Alana scribbled on a piece of paper and folded it into a tiny, origami frog. With infinite care – for she had to time its launch with a *creak*, a *click*, a *clack* or a *smack* – she aimed carefully and stroked the paper frog's back. Its legs shot forwards and up, so that it landed on Miller White's desk.

Wot u in 4? Miller read.

Miller checked Mrs. Snell wasn't watching and then leaned over to borrow one of the many pens wedged behind Colin Johnson's ears to answer. With care, he refolded the frog and flicked it back with equal accuracy.

Miller: *Chris thot gud idea 2 make lite saber.*

Alana: *So?*

Miller took a pen in a different color.

Miller: *Lab cot fire.*

Alana: *(@@)*

Miller shrugged and went back to reading his book.

Alana thought hard. She had really misjudged Miller. He wasn't slow at all, but really, really smart. Possibly even crazy.

He was perfect for her plan!

She bit her lip and wrote furiously.

Alana: *?4U. Can u hack in2 skool comp?*

Miller looked furtive before writing his answer.

Miller: *MayB.*

Alana: *911.*

Alana turned on her Puppy Dog Eyes to show this was a Real Emergency. Miller looked uncomfortable.

Miller: *OK.*

Alana could barely contain her excitement. She had one last idea she wanted to try on her own, but if that didn't work, at least now she had Miller. Finally, she might find out who Flynn really was, whether he was a Second-Chancer, and what, if anything, was his crime.

Alana: *Orsm! Details l8r dude.*

Back and forth the little frog had hopped – written on and refolded, as silent as a moth and yet ...

The two students were so engrossed in their private dialogue they failed to notice the absence of a *creak, click, clack* or *smack*. Or the sudden appearance of Mrs. Snell's little friend Silence.

"Peace and Quiet. Not too much to ask, I would have thought. And some people *still* find it hard!" the old woman said to Alana, shaking her head.

The paper frog, scribbled over and over with different colored pens, had made its final journey, but was nowhere to be seen. Alana sat with all the stillness of a rabbit deciding its next move against a snake. *Where could the paper frog have gone?*

Mrs. Snell broke eye contact with Alana and whipped her head to face Miller. "Isn't that right, Mr. White?" she whispered with a nasty gleam to her eye.

The teenager, cheeks bulging suspiciously, let out a croak.

"*Ribbit?*"

With a roll of her eyes and a muttered, "Fool!" Mrs. Snell shuffled closer ... and closer ... and then *past* their desks until she reached the two seniors, who were so caught up in each other they didn't notice her approach.

"So cozy. So cute. Young Love," she sneered.

"I was young once." Mrs. Snell sighed with real regret.

"Yes, but which century?" Miller wondered aloud. Alana stifled a giggle.

The strident call of the bell sounded, marking the passing of another hour – and the end of detention. There was a rush for the door.

"Not so fast, dearies. You," she said, pointing a long knitting needle at Colin Johnson, causing his ears to blossom a deep shade of red, "can leave the little drawings you've been working on, on my table." Colin gulped. Alana hoped, for his sake, they weren't the usual caricatures that were so cruelly accurate. "And you two," she fixed her beady eyes on the seniors, "I shall see again tomorrow … in SEPARATE classrooms! And you," she said, suddenly grabbing Chris Kruger by the collar, "should know better than to stick foreign objects up your nose." With three hard taps of her Size 8 knitting needle against his nostril, the offending jelly bean fell to the floor with a *plink*! "I have no doubt that I shall see both of *you* again," Mrs.

Snell said meaningfully to Alana and Miller, who walked backwards, slowly and calmly, until they reached the door ... and then ran full-speed up the stairs.

As Alana neared the top of the landing, she could hear the strident wail of a siren. It was loud and piercing – almost human in its despair. A long, red fire engine screamed past the school. A second one followed. Alana watched both trucks tilt on two wheels as they careened around a corner. The tall column of smoke caught her attention next. A line of dirty thumbprints on the city skyline.

"I wonder what's on fire?" Alana wondered aloud.

A small boy from Year Seven scurried past. "Somebody said it's St. Bernadette's College," he yelped.

One look at Miss Beatrice – formerly of the Benedictine Sisters and St Bernadette's College itself – confirmed it. She was sobbing hard as Coach Kusmuk patted her awkwardly on the shoulder. Miss Beatrice clutched the edge of Coach

Kusmuk's tracksuit top to wipe her eyes and then blow her nose. She gave a loud *honk*.

"Thank you, my child," she sniffed, releasing the sodden clothing. Coach Kusmuk stiffened.

Alana backed away quickly before the coach could find another reason to put her on detention.

CHAPTER 17

The sounds of music

The autumn sky was gray and gloomy. Leaves that had deepened to the reds and oranges of the season were turning brown and crinkly at the edges. The sky matched Alana's mood. It was the kind of mood that demanded loud guitar riffs, harsh chords, and a wicked, deep bass. Alana didn't want to dwell on why she was feeling this way. She just needed to clear her head and play guitar.

"...my fa-vorite things –" a voice warbled. Miss Beatrice, red-eyed and snotty, was strumming an acoustic guitar. Alana backed out of the music rehearsal room as quietly as she could, but not quickly enough. "Oh, Alana," Miss Beatrice's face lit up, "do come in."

"Sorry. Didn't know anyone was in here," Alana apologised.

"That's okay," Miss Beatrice gave a watery smile. It made her eyes look like the surface of a goldfish bowl. "I'm working through some ... angst. I find music *such* a comfort, don't you? Some people jog, others punch a bag, but I like to sing."

Alana smiled. "Yeah, me too. I often come here to blow off some steam. Guitar helps me think straight. Sometimes I like to write songs. What were you singing?" she asked.

Miss Beatrice gave a little laugh and looked embarrassed. "Oh, just a little ditty about all my favorite things. It comes from a musical that was very popular a long time ago. A real classic. Back in those days people didn't go around setting fire to, to, to," she gulped and took a deep breath to wail, "schools!" Alana patted Miss Beatrice on the shoulder, taking care not to stand too close in case the teacher got any ideas. Miss Beatrice made a big effort to regain her composure, and dried her eyes. "You must think me very foolish and sentimental. Tell me more about these songs you write. What are they about?"

Alana opened her notebook to show the teacher her songs.

"*Dream On. To There and Back. Whatever.* Hmm, they're very creative titles," Miss Beatrice said with false cheer. "It looks like we share a love of music."

There was a long silence.

Alana took back her notebook. "Well, I'll let you get back to your favorite things, Miss Beatrice. I'll come back later."

"You don't have to go," Miss Beatrice cried. "We could..." a soft rose color flooded her cheeks, "...sing together?"

"No offense, but I don't really, exactly ... like musicals." Alana suppressed a shudder with difficulty.

"You wouldn't have to. We could come up with a list of our own favorite things. Maybe set it to some rock? Work in a guitar solo or two?" she smiled winningly, hands clasped as if in prayer.

Alana shrugged. She supposed she'd done stranger things. And this definitely fit in with her New Year's resolution of doing something different every day. Alana found a seat and got her pen ready. They took turns to contribute lines to the song while Alana experimented with different sounds on the guitar. Miss Beatrice hummed the melody as she wrote and was already looking chirpier. Alana felt her own mood lighten despite herself. The first draft of their composition looked something like this:

Miss Beatrice: Book-swaps, composers, and winters in Britain,

Alana: Bright gerbera petals and songs that I've written,

Alana: Rock, Jimi Hendrix, and my guitar strings.

Miss Beatrice and Alana: This is a list of our favorite things.

Miss Beatrice: Fluffy, pink pom-poms, and cute-looking poodles,

Alana: Soccer, photography, weird, funny doodles,

Miss Beatrice: Musicals, Broadway, the songs that we sing.

Miss Beatrice and Alana: This is a list of our

favorite things.

[Guitar solo]

Alana: When I miss Dad,

Miss Beatrice: ... and St. Bernadette's,

Miss Beatrice and Alana: When we're feeling down,

Miss Beatrice and Alana: We just have a look at our Favorite Things List,

Alana: And then we don't need to drown.

"You know I'm all for a bit of melodrama, but how about we change that last word to 'frown'?" Miss Beatrice suggested.

Alana nodded her okay and then put her foot on the distortion pedal. She leaned back and readied herself on the guitar. "From the top?"

Maddie closed the door of the music room gently. "I don't know, guys," she confessed to Sofia and Khalilah, who were waiting outside. "I reckon if we tell Alana that the school Coach Kusmuk was going to transfer to has burned down, it might send her over the edge."

Another school fire?!

CHAPTER 18

Playing with fire

The matches were forbidden. The boy's dad had made that very clear. It wouldn't hurt just to touch them, though, he thought. The boy, just eight years old, reached out a hand and eased one of the sticks out of the box. Flimsy, he would have said if he'd known the word. They didn't look powerful. Or scary. Or something that could hurt. No harm to light just one, was the boy's next thought. He scratched it against the rough edge of the tiny box, hearing the rasp, feeling the suck of air. The acrid smell of chemical filled his tiny nostrils before a flame burst out – impossibly bright and hot. The boy dropped the match, suddenly frightened. The flame died. Silly, he admonished himself. It's not scary. He reached for the box again.

Hours, or was it minutes later, the boy had no idea, the boy's father returned. But the boy didn't hear him come – caught in the wonder of making magic. Hundreds of charred slivers, twisted and deformed, lay where he'd dropped them. Evidence of the boy's confidence. His confidence was snuffed out as quickly as the flare, though, the instant his father drew near. The boy could feel the heat of the man's anger. His father removed his belt. For the boy it was almost a relief. The angry man was better than the empty husk, the shadow, the memory of the man who'd been wandering the house, unaware his son was still there. You see me now, don't you, the boy said to his dad in his head. You see me now.

Right from the beginning, the boy was fascinated by fire. That there was so much power in something so tiny was a miracle. And that he could create it amazed him. Even more incredible was that he could control it. Such power, such control was the exact opposite to life at home. For if it had been up to him, his mother would never have left and he'd have one of those Perfect Dads on TV that played cricket with The Kids. Relaxed. Grinning. White-toothed. The day the boy's mother walked out, his dad had donned a thick overcoat he never took off again. Stiff. Impenetrable. Cold. It didn't let any feelings in. Or out.

When the boy became the Fire-Starter, he finally had a coat of his own.

CHAPTER 19

All fired up

Sofia's bedroom was as small as a cupboard. In fact it was a cupboard – a very generous storage space under the stairs – until it was converted into a bedroom for one of the six Luciano children. The three-bedroom home, unlike Alana's, was a squeeze for the family of eight. With Carlo and Monte at university, however, Sofia finally felt like she could breathe. A single mattress took up most of the floor. A small "shrine" displaying her good luck talismans had replaced the collection of dumbbells belonging to the room's former occupant. As well as a poster of Jet Tierbert which took pride of place where the centerfold from *Monster Muscles* had once hung. Electric drum pads sat in one corner and a strip of gauzy chiffon trimmed with bronze medallions hung down from the ceiling to hide her clothes. As the only girl, Sofia was grateful for the privacy Carlo's former bedroom provided. She was getting too old to share a room with Dmitri (brother number three), the twins, Pepe and Bob, and their collection of stinky socks.

"Did you know that there are at least three thousand firewalking instructors?" Sofia informed her friends. The spate of school fires had ignited her usual thirst for macabre facts.

"There are *schools* where you can learn to walk through fire?" Khalilah asked with wide eyes.

"Don't tell Coach Kusmuk that, whatever you do. Otherwise we'll be walking on hot coals next, rather than balancing beams. I heard she's getting advice from the military for her obstacle course designs." Maddie grimaced. "Apparently hurdles, quicksand, and climbing frames are way too tame."

Alana rolled her eyes. "As long as she doesn't team up with Mrs. Snell," she said. "That woman has artifacts I reckon a few museums in France don't know are missing."

The four girls were hunched over their mandala designs for art class. Positive thoughts, wishes, or statements of gratitude were written in very small, squashed handwriting, round and round in circles. Their art teacher – unlike Ling Ling, who had absorbed only the *colors* of Buddhist spirituality – had spent time with some *real* Tibetan monks and was now convinced that art should be a vehicle for World Peace and Optimism.

"I don't actually mind world peace," said Maddie, leaning back and rubbing her eyes. "I mean I've got nothing against it, but it's giving me an awful headache." It occurred to her that world leaders probably felt the same way. The positive words that Maddie had chosen to write were "infinite success" – she had a Grade Six violin exam coming up and she was determined to get a good grade.

Khalilah looked down at her colorful artwork, pleased with her efforts. She'd gone for the ultimate in positive thinking and penned a statement of gratitude for something that *hadn't happened yet*. "Thank you for my six-pack," she wrote in tiny, round letters that sat side-by-side like a rainbow of beads.

So far, Sofia calculated she had written the words "good luck forever" 358 times, and was still only halfway, which was why she put her pen (*grape-scented, delicious*) down and began passing her finger through the flame of a candle.

Khalilah shuddered. "Ooh, don't do that, Sofia," she cried, horrified and fascinated at the same time.

"It doesn't hurt," Sofia said, "see?" And she passed her finger through again (not the one with the mood ring, obviously) only this time more slowly, like a daredevil stunt rider who has added another semi-trailer to the jump.

Maddie welcomed the excuse for a break. "Let me have a go," she said, finally succumbing to the blurriness of her eyes. "infinite success" was being written as "intifite succceess" and she wasn't sure if that counted.

Khalilah gripped Alana's hands so that she had to stop and watch too. All three girls were spellbound as, with the lights off, Maddie's long, thin finger made its daring journey through fire, her face a semi-circle of reflected gold.

"Does it hurt?" Khalilah asked.

"Nah," Maddie shrugged. "You try."

Khalilah shook her head. "No thanks, not me." In her mind she was imagining the school fires – thankfully nobody had been hurt – and the damage and destruction they had caused. The photographs in the newspapers painted a grim picture – melted filing cabinets so deformed on one side that they looked like a Salvador Dali painting; charred books and ashes in piles, all that was left of a school library; and the huddle of distraught students. Fire was not something she felt like playing with.

A thought struck. "If you had sixty seconds to save one thing from a fire, what would it be?" Khalilah asked.

Maddie pulled her finger from the flame. "My violin," she said without hesitation.

Sofia pulled a face. "Just one? Well, Nostradamus, obviously." Thinking that there was nothing more important to her than the mongrel she'd rescued from "death's door" seven years ago ... apart from her lucky charms and amulets ... and her drumsticks ... and the autographed Jet Tierbert T-shirt ... "How about three? Surely in one minute we have time to grab *three* things?"

Khalilah smiled. "Okay. Three things then. What would you choose apart from Nostradamus?"

"Well," said Sofia, ticking the choices off her fingers, "I wouldn't take Nostradamus because of course Mom or Dad would bring him, so I would choose my lucky charms – all of them, because they fit quite comfortably around my neck if I'm not watching tennis – my drumsticks and my favorite T-shirt," she said, fondly stroking Jet's unprotesting face in printed 100% cotton. "What about you?"

Sushi, her portly pet cat, Khalilah said, would be on the top of her list because her mom would be too busy saving her research and her dad his massive camera and its 52 accessories. She would also rescue her pillow and diary. "Although," she wondered aloud with an enigmatic smile, "there are probably secrets in there others would want burned." This of course made the others desperately curious as to what the secrets were, and whether they knew any of them. "Of course," she lied, "you're my best friends and I tell you everything. Alana's turn. What would you take?"

Alana sucked on her pen thoughtfully. "I'd take my mom," she said after a while, "because she'd be so busy rescuing everything else, she'd forget to get out of the house."

The voice of Sofia's dad calling them for dinner and the thundering footsteps that followed, reminded the girls that they had better hurry. Sofia's twin brothers, Pepe and Bob, were not averse to lying, cheating or swindling anybody out of their food if it was left on the table for too long.

Alana followed after the others. Her mandala – "mystery solved" – would have to wait.

CHAPTER 20

Alana delves deeper

Emma had interviewed presidents and political activists. She had dined with rebels and rock stars. She'd even spent time up a tree in the jungles of Borneo being groomed by a 70-kilo orangutan! Yet somehow she couldn't string two words together whenever she had to speak with Dr.-Gray-please-call-me-Oliver. Whenever she tried, her tongue felt like it had been stung by a bee. Dr.-Gray-please-call-me-Oliver stood by the entrance of the Second-Chancer's room, one arm against the door frame, looking very Buff. "Buff" – Khalilah had informed her – was what she hoped to be when she got older. "You know, lots of muscle, toned, ripped –," Khalilah explained, biting into her third cream bun of the day. "I'm working on my six-pack now." She poked her stomach. "It's in there somewhere."

Emma had the feeling Dr.-Gray-please-call-me-

Oliver had a six-pack. By the look of him, probably even more. His arms were practically bursting out of his T-shirt to make their own introduction. Emma gave him a quick, small smile. For the second time she tried to explain how she felt about dating.

"You see," Emma said, dodging his amused eyes to drop her gaze to his lips and then seeking refuge in the ceiling, "I haven't been in the saddle for many years and I know that once you ride a bike you never forget how to, but it's been a long time." At this, she looked Dr. Gray in the eye and said intensely, "and I mean, a *very* long time," she faltered, "since I had a ... ride." She could tell it wasn't going well. He was laughing at her now. She was mixing up her idioms like her mother did and was Botching It Up. She tried again. "But I know it's time to get back on the horse again, and have another go. I'd just," she paused, "like to take it slow." She looked at him pleadingly.

Dr. Gray's eyes crinkled even deeper. "*Neigh*," he whinnied softly, causing her to blush.

Chapter 20

The raucous entrance of the Second-Chancers saved Emma from replying.

"Hey, it's the doc," cried Trần. "Hey, Doc, how you been, man?"

Dr. Gray straightened up, startled, but recovered himself and greeted the group with a friendly wave. Boris was even more excited. "Whoa, Doc, that low-carb diet you're on is really paying off. You think mine will get there soon?" Boris pushed up the sleeves of his leather jacket and flexed arms the size of matchsticks. The others laughed and pushed him away.

"Hey, can you do that muscle thing again where you make a mouse jump from one arm to the other?" Trần begged. "You know, when you go like this," Trần flexed his biceps to demonstrate, "and make this part of your muscle go down, while it pops over to the other side. It's so cool, Miss Emma," he enthused, "you have *got* to see it."

Emma fought back a smile while the others rallied around Dr. Gray, urging him to do the trick. Dr. Gray whipped his T-shirt off and then flexed a bicep until one small muscle seemed to bulge over the others. There were gasps of appreciation. With ease he turned his attention to the other bicep and made a similar bulge just as the original disappeared. Dr. Gray did it again. And again. Up popped a muscle in one arm, down popped another. It *did* look like a tiny mouse scampering under the surface of his skin. Soon all of the boys were topless, trying to outdo each other. Trần clenched his teeth and squeezed, but only a very slight curve appeared. Enzo's show of muscle was more impressive, but thwarted by his waistline. Boris *harrumphed* and *hawed*, but the effort only made his ribcage seem even hollower.

Emma watched Dr. Gray pull his T-shirt back on. "I'm happy to take it as slowly as you need," he whispered in her ear. His breath was warm. It tickled her hair.

"O-kay," Emma looked up, and nodded, dry-mouthed. "Slow. Good." She noted absentmindedly that his nostril hair was perfectly trimmed.

Dr. Gray's eyes were drawn to her half-open

mouth. Their color darkened into deep pools of liquid jade. "You've got great teeth," he whispered. "A few signs of tooth decay. But nothing a bit of regular flossing couldn't cure."

What? Emma shook her head. *For a minute she thought he was going to whisper Sweet Nothings about her lips or something! Did she just hear him giving dental advice?*

With a chuckle, Dr. Gray left.

Minutes later, there was a knock at the door. It was Alana. Three pairs of eyes swiveled to stare. Alana looked around the room of topless boys in various bodybuilding poses, struggling to display some form. She closed her eyes. She opened them. They were still there, still posing and *still* half-naked. What was her mom up to now?

"Hey, Miss Emma, is this hot chick your sister?" Boris asked, waggling a bushy mono-brow while he tried even harder to flex his muscles.

Alana looked affronted. "She's my *mom*, *imbécile*."

"Alana!" Emma hurried over to see what Alana

wanted.

But Boris, far from being offended at being called an idiot in French, was rather chuffed to have been given a special nickname. True, he didn't know what the word *imbécile* meant. Nevertheless it made him feel flattered that Miss Emma's hot-looking daughter had singled *him* out.

"Hi, Mom," Alana lowered her voice, "I was wondering if I you knew how I could join the kickboxing program?"

"Kickboxing? I didn't know you were interested."

"Interested?" Alana scoffed. "I love kickboxing! It's the most exciting sport ever," she lied. Alana was determined to see for herself whether Flynn was a Second-Chancer or not.

"You can't join kickboxing," Enzo said, eager for a unique "nickname" too. "That's just for people like us." He puffed his chest importantly.

"She can join ... if she knows the right people," Boris argued. He made an extra effort and tensed his muscles again, straining like a constipated peacock. Only his eyes bulged.

"You mean the wrong ones."

"Hold on, hold on," Emma interjected with a frown. "I really don't think this is the time or place to discuss enrollment in a sport that has the words 'kick' and 'boxing' in it, Alana. Can we talk about this at home?"

Alana gave a shrug of acquiescence and turned to go.

"You could probably catch some kickboxing now. They should still be in the ring," Trần called out helpfully.

"Great! You're the Man," Alana said, shooting him a grateful glance before running off.

Trần almost floated away with pride. "Did you hear that? I'm the Man. Trần-the-Man."

Boris refused to relinquish his crown. "Yeah, but *I'm* the Imbécile."

It only took a few minutes for Alana to reach the ring in the gym, but by the time she got there, someone looking very much like Flynn had already reached the exit. Alana barely caught a glimpse of the familiar hunch of shoulders before the boy disappeared. Alana launched forward, but upon reaching the door, she saw him already jogging down King Street, as if he knew she was in pursuit. Alana put Coach Kusmuk's back-breaking training to use and pelted after him. Past the souvlaki takeout, past the coffee shop, past the Body Builder's Gym. But Flynn – who was also Elite Squad – had a decent head start. After a sudden twist and turn past the florist and church hall, he was lost from sight.

"Im-possible," Alana wheezed, doubled over, panting. "He was just (*pant*) here (*pant*) a minute ago. (*Pant, pant, pant*). I swear it." But there was nobody who looked remotely like Flynn on the streets. There were just a few college students, a girl on a skateboard, and two women with tattoos and piercings putting up posters for a gig. Alana looked around, continuing to pant hard as she caught her breath. *Where could he have gone?* Now there was nothing for it. She would have to hack into the school computer with her new buddy Miller if she wanted to find out the truth about the mysterious Flynn.

Back at the Police Boys' Club, the sound of panting could also be heard. But it was no longer the panting of frustration or exertion. It was the panting of excitement as Trần, Enzo and Boris (with shirts back on) gave their presentation. The three youths were confident they were on the right track with their Team Building project. Their scheme satisfied every point Emma had explained. Yes, the project utilized their unique talents. Yes, they each had a special job they were required to do. Yes, it was vitally important to work together and cooperate for the project to succeed.

"So while Enzo guards the door, and Trần is waiting in the car, I says, 'Give me all the money in the till,'" panted an excited Boris, as he paused dramatically and looked around the room, "*please*," and with a roar of approval from his new team mates, nodded his head in self-congratulation.

CHAPTER 21

Stranger than fiction

Dr. Gray was true to his word and did not push for a second date. He took things very slowly – two months! – and Emma began to worry. Two months. A lot can happen in two months. You can buy your first comic book. You can discover you don't like okra. You can try online gaming and create "Maggie," who is invincible with a slingshot. You can start blogging and then stop because you keep forgetting your password. Emma knew exactly what could happen in two months. She was pretty sure she was now ready for a date, especially as Dr. Gray's brand new motorbike had been delivered to the Second-Chancers' room at the Police Boys' Club. Ordinarily, she disliked showy displays of wealth and power, but this *was* a Harley Davidson.

"He has a Harley Davidson?" Katriona and Ling Ling had squealed.

"What kind? Is it a DYNA Glide, Softail, Touring, VSRC, or Sportster? Low Rider? Night Train? Road King? Screamin' Eagle? Night Rod? What does it look like?" Katriona cried. With Tony from Tony's Tattoos as a friend, it was little wonder she was something of an expert.

Emma laughed. "I don't know. All I know is it was very wide and low and shiny."

"Probably a Fat Boy, then," Katriona sniffed with authority. "You're going out with a real bad boy!" Ling Ling nodded her approval.

"Anyway, he signed for his Harley and then he said the weirdest thing ..." Emma continued.

Her friends leaned forward eagerly, "What did he say?"

"He said, 'I'm not riding that!' Then, when I looked at him strangely, he said, 'I mean, it'll mess up my hair.' And when I looked at him even *more* strangely, he grabbed my hand and said, 'Forget it! Life's too short not to live dangerously.'" She paused. "Then we sat on his bike ..."

Katriona and Ling Ling gripped hands in

excitement, "Yes?"

"... and we *pretended* to ride his Harley ... through Mexico."

"What?!"

"Yep, he made all the sound effects and everything. Next time," she said with disgust, "he wants me to bring my *sombrero*."

"Never mind, never mind. Relak, relak lah," Ling Ling assured her, massaging Emma's tense shoulders. She eased Emma down with soothing noises until she was lying on her back on the daybed in her office. Emma reached into her bottle of painkillers and took one, chewing it in her anger. "At least," Ling Ling said over the sounds of Emma choking, "it gives us time to show you how to act properly on a date. Here," she clicked her fingers imperiously, "Katriona will show you how to walk."

Katriona looked away from her mirror with reluctance. She was sure there was another wrinkle near her eyes that wasn't there yesterday. She could almost *feel* herself aging. Katriona gave her skin a reassuring pat and dropped the hand mirror to her side as she demonstrated the Winning Walk.

"Note, shoulders back," Ling Ling pointed as Katriona walked. "Chin high, but not too high. Chest out, but not, well ... do your best." Katriona glided around the room, taking time to check her face in the mirror every now and then for any change.

"What did you say you were going to do again?" Emma said suddenly. She eyed the plastic container, which contained an odd mixture she could only describe as "goo."

Ling Ling picked up the bowl and mixed the flecks of white, beige, and yellow into a paste. "It's a facial treatment we read about. Based on an ancient Asian tradition," she lowered her voice. "Very popular with all the Stars of Hollywood." She proceeded to smooth the mixture onto Emma's face as Katriona continued to strut. "Many Chinese believe that bird-nest soup is good for cell growth and tissue repair."

At this, Emma sat up. Startled eyes popped out

of the ghoulish mask which looked like yellowing cement. "What do birds have to do with it?"

Ling Ling was prevented from answering by a loud yell from the door. It was Alana, and she wasn't alone.

"*Ergh!* What ith that awful thmell?" Alana complained, pinching her nose.

A boy about the same age as Alana and from the same school – judging from his uniform – followed her in. He was a curious-looking boy with strangely-positioned eyes and odd-shaped glasses. He walked past the enormous plastic Christmas tree as if it was normal bedroom décor for July. That it was covered with random bits of paper and torn napkins didn't bother him either. Perhaps he too used a plastic Christmas tree, year-round, as a place to put ideas, like Emma did. (In truth, he used a conventional whiteboard and plastered it with formulas.) The boy walked up to Ling Ling and dipped his pinkie in what remained of the mixture. He tapped it with staccato delicacy onto the tip of his tongue and alternately licked and smacked his lips, as if to test both taste and texture.

"Hmm, just as I thought," the boy said with a look of deep concentration. "I detect nitrogen, phosphate, and potassium."

"What-ium?" asked Alana.

"You'd probably call it bird poop."

"Bird WHAT?" cried Emma, sitting up.

Ling Ling pushed Emma back down. "Re-lak! This is a facial treatment traditional *kabuki* actors and geishas use. It is a very ancient beauty secret from the Orient."

But Emma refused to be pacified. She knew her friends all too well.

"I know the treatment, but the Japanese use powdered *nightingale* droppings which they sterilize first. Which bird did you use, Ling Ling?"

"Nightingale, parakeet, same-same lah!" the woman scoffed.

Katriona turned on Emma, furious. "The least you can do is to help me find a cure for aging. Look at me! I'm getting older every day!"

Alana smacked her head in disbelief before

leading Miller to the living room, where the sounds of the argument were not as loud. "I'll introduce you later," she said. "They're a bit busy."

Miller got down to work. While he tapped on the keys of the laptop, Alana couldn't help but express her curiosity.

"If you can do all this amazing stuff, how come you don't act brainy at school? Aren't you in the bottom class for math or something?"

Miller peered at the screen and muttered. "You learn pretty quickly that people who are 'brainy' aren't always the most liked. In fact, lots of people feel threatened. I mean," he paused, looking up, "if they're *the teacher*, you'd think they'd want to learn something new. But maybe they just aren't interested in nano-technology. As Gran says, it's not everyone's cup of tea – although I don't see what a beverage has to do with it. Anyway," he said, returning to the screen, "Practical math gives me time to study advanced calculus and be with my friends, Chris and Colin."

"That's really ... smart," Alana said admiringly.

Alana knew a bit about the downside of being "brainy" as well.

When Alana Oakley was born, and the months had chased each other, words were absorbed like a sponge. *Mom, dad, book, bird, cup.* Hot on their heels came *splashing, beautiful, different.* Then *peculiar, entrancing, dejected* followed.

They had to move the precocious preschooler to Miss Tate's class, if only to give Mrs. Rineheart the pre-retirement year she felt she'd earned. Surely, after 40 years of faithful service, she didn't deserve to have her grammar corrected by a *three year old!* Thus Alana was not only reading *See Spot Run* and *See Spot Run with Jill*, she was rewriting the story too. In careful handwriting, one arm clutching her blankie while sucking on a pacifier, *Spot and Jill wer scoring goles and eeting deelishus is creem* because that was far more exciting. It never occurred to her that the spaces between lines were deliberate. The *Spot and Jill* stories were like a join-the-dot or coloring page that needed filling in. Alana obliged – to the alarm of her teachers and the delight of her dad. Her grandmother was even more elated. According to Alana's grandmother, nobody was good enough for her daughter, Emma. To be Good Enough, you had to carry a laptop or briefcase, and be too busy to have a conversation without being interrupted by Important Phone Calls and Urgent Texts. They most certainly did not carry a *djembé* or call people "Dude." She wasn't impressed that Hugo had done both. But as soon as it was discovered Hugo had taught Alana to read (*clever, clever girl*), he went from being a good-for-nothing-no-hope-bongo-drum-player to my-son-in-law-the-genius. Thus Alana was able to win the scholarship to Gibson High, but in order to *keep* it, she had to maintain high grades. It was mainly for this reason that she worked so hard at school.

"I'm sorry. Your laptop – while a very charming shade of turquoise – is inadequate for the purposes of infiltrating the firewall of the school's computer system and deciphering their encryption. May I suggest we redeploy to somewhere more suitable?"

Miller said, peering over his glasses.

"Huh?"

"Do you want to come over?"

"Oh. Sure."

The bang of the front door and a muffled, "Be back soon" interrupted Emma, Katriona, and Ling Ling's bickering.

After a heartbeat, Ling Ling asked, "Did Alana just bring home a *boy*?"

"No," Katriona said, peering through the curtains, "Alana just *left* with a boy."

Emma stared at her two friends and lay back down. "Oh, very well," she huffed, "give me the Works."

...

Ling Ling watched with envy as Katriona tilted to the left, a swathe of long fair hair cascading down to her thigh. With a *screech*, Katriona tipped suddenly to the right, leaning back as she did so. Katriona shook her head in exhilaration.

She could almost smell the gas fumes. Ling Ling tapped her foot with impatience. Both she and Katriona had dressed up for this special occasion. Ling Ling had swapped Buddhist spiritualism for Soho spunk and was decked head-to-toe in bright orange leather, while Katriona wore leopard-skin tights and a studded leather jacket.

"My turn now," Ling Ling demanded.

"*Brmm. Brmm. Brrrrrmm.* Just a bit longer," Katriona whined.

Ling Ling tugged at Katriona's hands, which gripped the bike's throttle. "Come on, you've been on for ages."

"NO! I said. Just. A. Bit. Longer!" Katriona held the Harley in a death grip between her thighs.

The *clang* of a mop bucket and the *thunk* of the light switch in the basketball court next door interrupted their scuffle.

"Take your finger out of my eye, Katriona," Ling Ling whispered. "I think somebody's here."

The cleaner of the Police Boys' Club was surprised to find a Harley Davidson in the Second-

Chapter 21

Chancers' room. He was even more surprised to see a woman's lipstick print on the shiny chrome of the bike's mirror. "I guess this one's a female," hc shrugged.

CHAPTER 22

Flynn under the microscope.
Road rage.

News of Coach Kusmuk's disaster-struck future school did not improve anybody's mood – least of all Alana's. It looked like the coach would remain at Gibson High for another year at least.

"It just got personal," Alana said with a fierce glint in her eye.

Alana was not the only one to become fascinated by the antics of what became known as the Toy Truck Arsonist. It became a hot topic at school, too. The fact that the criminal (or criminals) appeared to be targeting schools, and left a toy truck at each crime scene, had everybody wondering who it could be. The press took to writing sensational reports, even though the police remained tight-lipped about their progress. The question on everybody's lips was: would their school be next?

But if the police were puzzled, what hope did

Alana have of solving yet another riddle on top of the mysterious Flynn, whose records had turned out to be disappointingly boring? He had recently transferred from out of state and, by the look of it, spent most of his life moving schools every one or two years. His father was Major Paul Tucker. There was no evidence of a mother, and he had one older brother.

"So there's nothing? Nothing at all on his record about misdemeanors? Suspensions? Expulsions? Nothing?" Alana cried in disappointment.

Miller looked up from his computer. "Nothing on record. Looks like a typical army brat. Moved around a lot, with stints in Haiti and Rwanda." Alana nodded. That would explain the French.

Flynn's lack of wickedness appeared conclusive until Alana overheard the deputy principal deliver a grave warning:

"The police are keen to pin these fires on someone, and your record isn't doing you any favors. If you cannot account for your whereabouts from four to six, then it doesn't matter what I or your teachers say. Flynn," he appealed, "we can't help you if you won't help yourself."

Flynn's eyes remained stubbornly glued to the floor.

"Very well. I expect I'll be seeing your father soon enough."

Flynn walked away, but not before spotting Alana, who could not duck behind the potted plant quickly enough. The scowl he gave her was as dark as thunder.

So that's the mystery of Flynn's school records solved, she thought to herself. Could all of these pieces be interconnected? Could Flynn Tucker be the Toy Truck Arsonist?

Alana's history teacher, Mrs. Snell, took advantage of the hot topic to describe gruesome, fire-related, historical details, the likes of which were guaranteed to give them all nightmares.

"Fire," Mrs. Snell said during one lesson, "has exacted its wrath throughout the course of humanity. In the year 1666, the heat from the Great Fire of London was so powerful that it made the lead roof on St. Paul's Cathedral drip like ice cream. According to eyewitness accounts, hundreds of pigeons preferred to brave the fires rather than abandon their nests. Their wings burned and they plummeted, down, down, down, to their deaths. *Aww*," Mrs. Snell smiled. "Poor things." Sofia fiddled with her mood ring – now a muddy yellow – and avoided eye contact. Mrs. Snell strolled around the classroom, needles a blur as her knitting trailed behind like a woollen tail.

"Witchcraft hysteria reached its peak in the sixteenth and seventeenth centuries. Common witch-hunting methods included drowning, leg vices, whipping stocks, and scalding lime baths." Khalilah put a shocked hand to her mouth, while Maddie, on the other hand, tried not to think of pond scum as she stared at the spittle in the "V" of Mrs. Snell's lips.

"But fire was also used as a means of torture to extract confessions from these so-called 'witches,' who were usually just kind, little old biddies good with herbs and healing." Mrs. Snell paused – a kind, little old biddie herself ... at least in her own mind. "Between 50,000 and 80,000 suspected witches were executed from 1500 to 1660. Eighty percent were women." Mrs. Snell's face swooped so Alana could see hairline cracks in the teacher's powdered cheeks.

"Tied to a stake and then, *whoomph*, set alight. If they survived, they were a witch and if they didn't, they were innocent!" She paused, eyeing Alana, a question mark in her eyes. Alana – like the "witches" before her, who knew they were doomed if they did and doomed if they didn't – remained rigid and silent. Mrs. Snell's hideous smile surfaced again, like a deep-sea monster. "Have you got anything to say to *that*, Miss Oakley?" she asked.

Why don't you ask Flynn? Alana thought to herself, but instead all she said was, "Poor things?"

...

As much as Alana would have liked another chance at tailing Flynn during the unaccounted-for hours, training for soccer, homework, and mid-year exams made it impossible. She was dwelling on the unfairness of it all – why couldn't she do this full-time? – when somebody gave her a poke. Hard.

"*Oww.*" Alana clutched at her side.

"You haven't been listening to a word," Khalilah accused.

Alana thought about lying but decided against it. Khalilah's radar for Stretched Truths and Embellished Tales was almost as sharp as Alana's radar for Mystery. Alana blamed her suspicious mind on her mother. Alana would be (happily) naive if Emma wasn't always Up To Something.

"Sorry, what were you saying?" Alana said apologetically.

"I was saying, I wish *I* could do that," Khalilah pointed.

The two girls were at Bondi Beach, legs dangling over the side of the path's edge, overlooking the sea. The coastal hotspot attracted hordes to its beach in the summers, but even the winters drew crowds.

Bondi was a favorite haunt of Khalilah's too, not only because of its freshly cooked fish and chips, cool rap music, and awesome graffiti art, but also because of the Bondi skate bowl.

The rumble of wheels against the concrete always made Khalilah's heart skip a beat. Skaters took turns freefalling from the lip of the basin to plunge into its cavernous depths (supposedly over 3½ meters deep) only to come up the other side and repeat the process. After the skateboarder had achieved enough momentum – and only if he or she was good enough – could they take off, grip their board and freeze in the air in suspended animation. Khalilah was fascinated by their daring displays of aerial mastery. It was a kind of magic, defying gravity.

"No reason why you can't learn," Alana pointed out.

"Me? With this body?" Khalilah scoffed.

"You can do anything you want to," Alana insisted. "If you really want to." And then Fate (if you believe in Fate) turned up – in the unlikely

form of a rather scrawny figure with six fingers –
not counting thumbs. It was Two-Fingered Trần,
or as he liked to introduce himself now, Trần-the-
Man.

"Hey! It's Hotchickalana!" he called out with a
wide grin, a beaten-up skateboard under his arm.

It wasn't long after the greetings and
introductions were made that Khalilah was
balancing on that very board with an equally wide
smile on her face. "Look! I'm doing it! I'm doing
it!" she cried excitedly. Khalilah was standing on
the skateboard, which was not moving, and had
not yet fallen off.

Alana left them to it, crossing over to the beach
side where a group of Japanese tourists were peace-
signing at a camera. She kicked off her shoes and
sank her toes into the soft sand. It was like sinking
into a warm, solid, shifting bath. The salty air
made her skin damp and clammy. The rhythmic
pounding of the surf provided the perfect
background for her thoughts – how to find out
where Flynn disappeared to for two hours every

day. So far the Mexican *sombrero* disguise hadn't worked, and chasing him down hadn't either... As Alana worked her way through options, she decided the simplest thing to do would be to hide, preferably in a vantage point, so she could see but not be seen. Since she had lost Flynn near the florist and church hall on King Street, the first floor of the café across the road – home to the Hare Krishnas – was her best bet, she thought to herself as she pounded a fist into her hand.

Alana's sudden cry of satisfaction frightened off a pair of gulls stalking her shoes in the hope that they were something edible. She dusted off her jeans to flick away the remaining grains of sand. By the time Alana walked back to Khalilah and Trần, Khalilah had mastered the "takeoff" as well as the "glide." Alana had never seen her look happier. "You did real good!" Trần was saying. "Let's do it again sometime," and then he began to show Khalilah his way of saying goodbye, which involved a strange hand movement to slick back his hair, bumping opposing shoulders on the diagonal, and wiggling fingers – or what remained of them – at each other.

"This is how we say goodbye in Brunei," Khalilah said demonstrating, stretching out both hands to clasp his in a handshake, and then bringing her own hands back to her chest. "It means that whatever good intentions you have in your heart, I place in mine," she explained.

"That's way cool," Trần exclaimed. "Like a heart-to-heart thing. Well, see you later!" and with a wave he was off on his skateboard to practice more double kickflips.

"Way cool," Khalilah echoed with longing. From the way Khalilah was staring at Trần's skateboard, Alana got the feeling her friend wasn't talking about their handshake.

But the day's excitement for Khalilah had only begun. As they left the skate park on their bicycles, a young driver in a Monaro wasn't looking where he was going and almost knocked her off. Khalilah wasn't a very experienced rider – truth be told, she was still getting the hang of riding the streets – but she knew when someone was in the wrong. The combination of fright, shock and self-righteous anger prompted a furious glare and rude hand signal. Then Khalilah rushed off to catch up to Alana, who was oblivious to the unfolding drama.

The young driver didn't appreciate being told off *in front of his friends* by someone younger than himself; and even worse, by a girl. With a screech of brakes, he tore after Khalilah to tell her so. It didn't take long for Alana to notice that the Monaro was blazing after them and that the driver was mad. The driver had already cut off two cars to inch its way further up Oxford Street to yell abuse.

"What's that guy's problem?" Alana asked Khalilah, who explained, in between labored breaths up the steep hill, about her near-death experience and the two-fingered salute. Khalilah had picked up more from Trần than the "takeoff" and the "glide."

Staying ahead of the Monaro was easier in some parts of Sydney than others. Alana and Khalilah's escape relied heavily on three factors:

their knowledge of back streets (not great), the traffic (quite heavy, so good), and their fitness (?!). Whenever they thought they had lost it, they would hear the roar of the souped-up engine and the thunderous exclamations from its exhaust, which sent their legs spinning faster. But after fifteen minutes of playing cat and mouse, Khalilah was tiring, Alana was running out of inspiration, and the Monaro wasn't giving up.

"Follow me," Alana yelled as a new idea struck. It was risky but it was their only chance.

Their bikes wove in and out, up and down, and sometimes missed pedestrians by centimeters when footpaths offered the only safe passage. Alana's circus-like horn came in handy. Its baritone bellow got people scuttling out of their way. Nevertheless, the Monaro got closer and closer. It was only after Alana and Khalilah turned into a quiet street that sloped gently downhill a couple of suburbs away that the Monaro screeched to a halt.

"Go! Go! Go!" the driver's friends urged from the backseat, baying for blood.

The driver peered up at the street sign – Eveleigh Street, Redfern – and muttered, "Nah, not worth it," before turning back, thwarted, in a cloud of burnt rubber and dirty exhaust.

The two bikes continued on more slowly and then one of them stopped. Alana looked back at Khalilah and said, "It's okay. I don't think they're going to follow us."

But Khalilah was looking, not up the road where the Monaro was driving away, but up at the sky where the thudding sound of a helicopter pulsed like an oversized heartbeat. "No, I know," she said, her face hopeful, "I was just wondering if we made it on *Speedsters*."

CHAPTER 23

A little respect

Road-rage drivers, it must be said, were not on Maddie's family's list of Favorite People, either. Nor were Volunteers with Good Intentions, as they were to find out that Saturday afternoon. Volunteer Sharon Morris sat primly on the edge of the proffered chair. She smoothed her skirt for the third time and looked around. The sea of expectant faces did not help her nerves. Despite her two-day course on "effective communication," she launched into the questionnaire that would determine what could be done to help without so much as a howdy-do, eager to be gone from what was reputedly Sydney's most violent neighborhood. That that dubious honor was actually held by another suburb made no difference to public perception. Wasn't life complicated enough without challenging *almost comforting* labels?

"So they're your half-brother and half-sister

then?" Sharon Morris asked Maddie, as she ticked boxes and scribbled notes in the margin. It brought to Maddie's mind a magician's box: as if her siblings had been sawn in two. The question made Maddie's mom bristle with anger – hadn't halves, quarters, eighths and other frightening fractions divided families for generations with society's obsession with blood and its subsequent dilution? Blood was blood was blood. And no amount of counting or note-taking would make Maddie, Troy, and Cassy feel any less like brother or sister. What infuriated her even more was that nobody ever asked any of the really important questions like, "How are you?" and *genuinely cared* about the answer they gave. Instead it was all business. Professional. And subsequently *cold*.

Uncle Joe was also in a grumpy mood. Sharon Morris had mistaken him for that old geezer, what's-his-face, down the road. The smelly one with the gimpy leg and missing teeth. Was the woman blind? They looked nothing alike, and Joe was at least ten years younger.

Running around pretending to be an aeroplane (or a very noisy bird) was four-year-old Troy, and (forever) trailing after was little sister, Cassy, a year younger. Neither of them knew they were half of anything as they ducked in and out of furniture, legs and potted plants, with Khalilah chasing them and making scary noises. Suddenly, Khalilah changed tack. She huffed and puffed to a stop, acting as if she was too tired. She collapsed on the couch in defeat, all the while keeping an eye out for the creeping figures, which tiptoed from behind. "Gotcha!" she yelled, pouncing as the pair squealed in fear and delight. The teenager tucked each child under an arm like sacks of potatoes. Their shaking and squirming produced a shiny, plastic packet from Troy's pocket. Khalilah put them both down to pick the sweets up from the floor. "*Mmmm!* Jelly babies. My favorite!" she said with a big wink. "I'm hungry, too."

Maddie's little brother snatched at the bag. "They're not jelly babies. They just look like it. Anyhow …" he added, in case Khalilah got any ideas, "they've got bacon in them."

Maddie's mom took in a shocked breath, but Khalilah just roared with laughter. "I don't like sharing my jelly babies either," she confided to him. With a suspicious glance backwards, Troy ran off, hand-in-hand with his little sister – but not before slipping a fat, red-sweet, half-melted, and squashed candy into Khalilah's hand.

Miss Morris took note of Khalilah who, although she bore no resemblance to the rest of the family, could well be a relative. She clicked her pen decisively. In her job it did not pay to assume. "And this is ...?" Sharon enquired with a vague wave in Khalilah's direction.

"Cousin," wheezed Uncle Joe promptly, ignoring Khalilah's surprise. Sharon Morris bent her head to tick yet another box.

When Sharon Morris took her leave to continue her survey elsewhere, Uncle Joe waved his arms like a baby bird attempting to fly. The saggy pockets of his biceps flapped like wash drying on the line.

"Hurry. Hurry. Help me up," he urged.

Chapter 23

"Where you going, then?" Maddie asked, flummoxed.

"I'm off," he said pointing to the house across the road. "I'll show that young Missy how alike we all look. Mess up those tidy numbers of hers," he grumbled.

Khalilah took his arm and helped the elderly man to the door. "I'll help, shall I?" she said with a cheeky grin, grabbing a cap to hide her braids. "Who shall we be this time?"

CHAPTER 24

Dating disaster

It wasn't *fractions* which were making life more difficult for Alana, but a different mathematical concept called algebra. The countdown to The Big Game was overshadowed by the mid-year exams, which ambushed Alana. At least that's what it felt like. No matter how hard she studied, she never felt it was enough. Alana knew she could just as easily ask help from Sofia who, under Mr. Hornby's nurturing tutelage, had turned into something of a mathematical whiz. But Sofia was tired of Alana's rants about keeping letters and numbers separate, like some kind of alpha-numerical apartheid. Besides, Alana enjoyed Skyping Uncle James for help, especially when he was in an exotic location, like now. While she wore double of everything – woolly beanie, pullover, and leggings – James was a world away in a T-shirt and shorts.

"Show me the Eiffel Tower again," she begged.

James had moved his webcam away from the iconic view after Alana had become too distracted. *The Eiffel Tower!* How many times had her father passed it as a youth?

"I'll show it to you *after* you've done question three," James promised.

Alana bent her head in concentration, then showed her work to the webcam before saying slyly, "Mom's out on a date tonight. With Dr. Teen Expert," in case James had forgotten.

Alana was not disappointed by James's reaction. The laptop in Paris fell, revealing the hotel room's ornate rococo ceiling. *Ooh la la! Extravagant!*

"Really?" James asked too casually, once he'd righted the screen. He adjusted it to include the view from the window as promised, as well as to hide from Alana's perceptive gaze.

"*Wow, il est si divine,*" Alana breathed. (Wow, it is so divine.)

"So where have they gone?" James asked, because he didn't care.

"Sofia's dad's restaurant, *Gastroniment,*" Alana

said distractedly. She was already jotting down ideas for a song. A song about Paris …

…

Emma was pleased about the choice of restaurant. She hadn't been to *Gastroniment* since it had first opened. In the restaurant's early days, family and friends alike had pitched in to lend Sofia's dad a hand, and Emma had helped by waitressing. Those days of struggling-to-make-ends-meet were gone. Now it was impossible to dine there without booking weeks in advance. *Gastroniment* continued to get rave reviews for its innovation and creativity.

Sofia's dad – owner and chef – was no ordinary cook. Luca Luciano was part of the "experimental cuisine movement" and his cooking style was a combination of science and art. Each meal excited the senses of sight, sound, smell, taste, and touch in different ways.

Emma was still pinching herself that she was

on a date (finally!) with Oliver, when a woman dressed as a traditional *geisha* greeted them at the door. The theme for tonight's meal was "*Trésors* of the Orient," which promised a fusion of French and Asian cuisine. Dr. Gray insisted she call him by his first name, and Emma had one chance to look briefly into the emerald depths of his eyes before being swallowed by the inky black of the restaurant's interior. An infra-red goggle-wearing "*ninja*" waiter led the way.

Emma clutched her favorite bag closer and rubbed the different textures of the patchwork fabric between anxious fingers. She knew she was prepared for this. Hadn't Katriona and Ling Ling made her practice her walk, over and over again? Wasn't she now proficient in the art of batting eyes and giggling genteelly into her hand? Plus she was sure she no longer spoke with a mouth full of food. All the same, she felt reassured that Katriona and Ling Ling were outside the restaurant window, ready to give her visual cues as to what to do.

The first thing Emma noticed was that she couldn't even see her hand in front of her face. In the darkness (was there a blackout?) her ears picked up the delicate notes of a Japanese harp. A firm but gentle hand guided her to a cushion, where she was invited to sit cross-legged on the woven floor. A hint of jasmine scented the air. Saturday night, the waiter informed them, was called "Blackout" because, in order to enhance the taste of the meal, diners *ate in the dark!*

Outside *Gastroniment*, Katriona and Ling Ling pressed their noses to the glass. They couldn't see Emma, but that didn't mean she couldn't see them. Perhaps it was one of those one-way-mirror thingies which guarded people's privacy. Katriona – with her vast experience of stalking – knew all about *those*.

"Let's just mime what she needs to do. She'll be able to pick it up as we go along," Katriona suggested. And so Katriona and Ling Ling went through their entire repertoire – to the delight of passing tourists, who stopped to watch the performance art.

Inside the restaurant – oblivious to her friends' efforts – Emma felt the table surface for the location of her cutlery, serviette and glass, almost knocking over the latter as she did so. A nervous giggle escaped like a bubble.

"You look lovely," Oliver said as soon as he sensed the waiter had gone.

It was pitch black. There was no way either of them could see each other, much less admire each other's looks. Emma appreciated Oliver's attempt to put her at ease with the gentle joke. She laughed, and then snorted. And then laughed because she'd snorted. And then laughed again. "I'm sorry," she said when she'd finally calmed down enough to take a breath. "I always make that horrible sound when I'm nervous."

Oliver's tone was serious as he felt across the table to hold her hand. "There's no need to be nervous." Then, as if he knew touching Emma might make her feel even *more* nervous, he dropped her hand and took a sip from his glass.

Emma heard Oliver take an exaggerated sniff, a noisy slurp, and then gargle for an unnaturally long time. "Hmm, a very delicate bouquet with citrusy overtones," he said with all the confidence of a professional sommelier. "I'd say ..." he paused to gargle again before declaring, "... a 1983 or '84 vintage, most likely from a mountainous area."

"Very astute, sir," an invisible waiter said by the pair's table. "Mount *Franklin* to be exact, with a slice of lemon. May I top up your *water*?"

The tinkle of water being poured into their glasses covered the sound of Emma's stifled giggle.

"Have you been to *Gastroniment* before?" an unfazed Oliver asked.

Emma welcomed the shift of topic as she took a sip. "Oh yes. I used to work here. As a waitress. I helped the owner when he first opened the restaurant. His daughter, Sofia, and mine have been best friends for years."

As if on cue, Sofia's dad, Luca, appeared by Emma's elbow. "Emma! I didn't know you were dining here. You should have warned me. I would have made... errr... special arrangements. Are you still vegetarian?"

"Luca!" Emma cried and then clumsily tried to kiss him on both cheeks but, in the dark, missed, and head-butted his nose instead. "I'm so sorry. Yes. I'm vegetarian, but don't worry. I'm sure everything will taste fantastic. It always does. This is Oliver, by the way," she said, waving in what she hoped was the right direction. Oliver reached out a hand blindly to shake Luca's hand but ended up punching him in the groin.

"*Oof*," Luca Luciano winced, doubling up. "Good to meet you, Oliver. It's always a pleasure to see you, Emma," he wheezed, before returning to the kitchen. Now Emma was not the only one feeling nervous. Luca Luciano could also feel his stomach tighten with worry. The last time he'd felt like this was when an important food critic had dined in his restaurant to write a review. As much as he adored the Oakley family, whom he'd known for years, he was well aware what a disaster Emma Oakley could be. Even though Luca had relied on volunteers in the beginning, he'd let Emma go (gently, of course) simply because she was bad for business. There was no way any chef could sell "crowns of lamb" if the waitress (Emma) told diners stories about Patches, the orphan lamb, hand-reared on a bottle. Luca shuddered, remembering distraught customers weeping at tables.

"Another organic vegetable risotto, please!" Emma had demanded cheerily of kitchen staff, who'd glared at her in disgust.

No. Emma Oakley caused bedlam and destruction wherever she went. It was all Luca Luciano could do not to sink to the floor, defeated. He forced himself to calm down and think rationally. Emma Oakley was simply here for a meal, and he was going to prepare the most delectable, mouth-watering, meat-free dish that France and Asia had to offer. A sense of calm returned. Until he heard the scream.

The appetizers placed on the table as a snack had ruptured Emma's troublesome tooth. At once the tooth went from bad to worse. Emma felt a warm wetness fill her mouth. Oliver brought out a dentist's flashlight – what kind of person has one of those? Oliver, obviously (!) – for a quick look.

"Arghhh! Blood! So much blood!" the diner sitting opposite them screamed when the light found Emma's face. Blood was gushing from her mouth.

The table next to them joined in. Lit by the flashlight, Emma's head appeared to float eerily as it dripped red gore. The dungeons of London didn't have anything nearly so grisly. There were more screams and then the rushing of feet and scraped chairs. People tripped over cushions and over each other, prompting more screams. Staff were pinned to the walls as customers charged past. A *ninja* waiter cowered in the corner.

"Looks like you'll need an operation," Oliver said, snapping the light off with a decisive click, oblivious to the stampede thundering past him.

"An operation?" Emma whispered before

fainting.

...

Luca Luciano looked around his restaurant. The lights were on. Two strange women were outside his restaurant enacting a pantomime. A siren, wailing in the distance, faded as an ambulance drove away. *Gastroniment* was empty, bloodied, and in a shambles.

Luca Luciano tore at what little hair he had left on his head and screamed.

...

When Emma came to, briefly before the operation, she saw Dr. Gray. The image swam as she dragged herself upright. "Oliver?" she mumbled.

"Yes?" Now it was the dentist from the clinic with the fighting fish – now dead, *sorry, terribly sorry* – who came to her bedside.

Emma gave a gasp of panic.

"You're going to be just fine. We're going to take out your wisdom teeth, and then they won't trouble you anymore."

"Teeth?" Emma shook her head to gain more clarity. "I only have *one* sore tooth."

"In for a penny, in for a pound, as they say," the dentist said, laughing jovially. "We may as well take them all out, since they'll only cause the same problem later. Better to do it in one go, don't you think?"

A thought seemed to dawn on her. "Who is *we*?"

"Dr. Gray and I. You won't feel a thing. We'll use general anaesthetic. You'll be completely unconscious when I unhinge your jaw so it can lie on your chest. That will give him," he gestured with a thumb at Dr. Gray, "lots of room to get in there."

Emma turned huge eyes to Oliver. She was pretty sure that just because you had the word "doctor" as a title, you weren't allowed to remove people's teeth willy nilly. "Are you mad? Have you even done this before?" she cried.

Before Oliver could answer, the dentist held up a comforting hand. "Yes, it *is* his first time, but rest assured, I'll be assisting and ..." he trailed off. Emma had fainted again. He was disappointed. He didn't even get to show her the most exciting bit, which was the large instrument they were using for the extraction!

CHAPTER 25

Dr. Jekyll and Mr. Hyde

The park's skyline, unlike other parks, was dominated by three tall, red-brick chimneys. From the top of the slides, children felt they could almost touch the chimneys, or at least measure themselves against them, like a height chart in the sky. Their laughter and cries spun in the air like cotton candy – muffled and sweet. Emma wandered around the playground, lost in a world where a much younger Alana had dug holes in the sandpit and hung upside down from the ropes of the web. Back to a time when Hugo had chased the two of them – screaming and giggling – in a monster version of tag.

"Arrgh. Arrgh. Monster come to get you! Monster come to eat you!"

Emma sat on a swing and kicked off gently, allowing the pull and tug of gravity to lift her into the air and back to Earth. She tipped her head back when she had enough momentum, and let her hair almost scrape the ground, watching the blue sky, white clouds, and brick towers sway into view and away again. Red. White. Blue. And then collapse in reverse. Blue. White. Red. Like the colors of the French flag. Why was it that everything reminded her of Hugo?

When she felt her momentum slow down, she used her feet to kick off again and took in deep breaths, expelling them loudly.

"Mommy," she heard a child's voice say loudly, "I wanna, I wanna ride onna swing."

"Shhh," was the reply, "Let the lady have a turn first."

Emma put her feet down and slowed to a stop – saddened that the ride had not helped her shake off the feeling that dating was not much fun. If anything, it had confirmed it. Going out with Oliver was just like the ride on a swing, with so many ups and downs that it made her feel queasy.

She had been appalled by her first dating

experience and shuddered at the memory of Jet's sweet young face. He was young enough to be her *child*, yet under the anonymity of online dating she'd treated him like a man. Emma surprised herself by even thinking of dating again. But as horrible as the experience had been, for a little while the online exchange revealed a flaw she hadn't even known existed. Like a slight crack in a china cup. There was a space in her heart now that couldn't be filled by her clever, beautiful, and talented daughter or her mad yet lovable friends, Katriona and Ling Ling, or even the work, which still thrilled and excited her every time she put pen (figuratively) to paper. It was a space not quite where Hugo had been (for nobody could ever replace Hugo), but somewhere very, very close.

But dating Dr. Gray was proving very confusing. It had been disappointing enough that he'd taken her on the date in his Volvo rather than the Harley. And she wasn't really impressed by his biceps – even if they did contain virtual mice. But it was the comments on not only *her* teeth, but *other* people's teeth, that really drove her to distraction. What was his obsession with *dentistry*?

"It's just a hobby," Oliver had assured her. And no, of course he hadn't operated on her. That, apparently, had been a hallucination. "Although, you know what? Whoever did the extraction did an incredible job, even if I do say so myself," Oliver said after inspecting her mouth.

Emma had been unable to resist venting her frustration to Alana and her three friends, who were over for a sleepover and anxious not to miss a word. "Do you know, sometimes I feel like I'm going out with two different men. One minute he's all charming, and interesting, and funny. The next all he talks about is teeth, teeth, teeth!" Emma stormed. Steam billowed around her like an angry cloud. She was wearing a towel wrapped around her head, a thick bathrobe embroidered with Nietzsche's advice to "Live dangerously," and fluffy bunny slippers. The eyes on the slippers hung by a thread, leaving Mr. and Mrs. Bunny looking demented.

"I can't even brush without feeling guilty. 'The gaps between your teeth –'" she said in a voice clearly imitating Dr. Gray's, "'are home to millions of bacteria, especially when particles of food become lodged there and begin to decay. Bad breath, tooth decay, gingivitis are all avoidable. All you have to do is floss.' Does any of that sound romantic to you?" she had asked the girls. "I mean, what kind of a person takes up dentistry as a hobby?!" All four gulped. They were relieved when Emma had flounced off without waiting for a reply.

Things were definitely weird.

"Maybe he's mentally unstable."

"Or on drugs. Drugs can do that to people, you know. It makes them go crazy."

"Or maybe," Sofia suggested hours later, as they huddled under a blanket on Alana's bed, with nothing but a flashlight shining eerily on their faces, "maybe *he's* the tall, dark, mysterious stranger my cousin, Erin, was talking about," she said dramatically, pushing the latest graphic novel she was reading into view.

The four girls stared at the title: *Dr. Jekyll and Mr. Hyde* by Robert Louis Stevenson.

"Yeah," Khalilah breathed, arms smothered in goosebumps, "The tall, dark, mysterious *psychic* stranger."

"You mean, 'tall, dark, mysterious *psychotic* stranger,'" Maddie said darkly.

Alana felt a familiar tingle in the back of her mind. Something wasn't right. In addition to the mystery of Flynn, it looked like she would have to investigate the weird personality of Dr. Gray.

Emma did not know of the girls' suspicions, although it may have offered some strange comfort if she had. As she wandered back home, lamenting the loss of the Sandringham Hotel (where Hugo and Emma had first met) along the way, and resisting the smells of restaurant food – Thai, Lebanese, Fijian – her thoughts spiraled downward into a Sad Spot. Why did things have to change? Just as quickly, she stopped herself. She knew from experience that after the question about Change came the question about Dying, and for that there was no answer.

At her front door, Emma patted her pockets and, disturbingly, found nothing. She emptied her handbag, from which she extracted a packet of tissues, sunglasses, peach-scented hand lotion, lipstick, a bottle of painkillers (now separated from the similar-looking bubble bath capsules), the-spare-change-from-a-jar-on-the-fridge, a baby tooth, a rubber band, scrap paper, a packet of half-eaten sweets (for diabetics, she said, because you could save a life with a well-timed jelly baby), a black pen, a skipping rope, a safety pin, and (because of Oliver) a toothbrush, just in case. More bizarrely, she found a flashlight, a butane torch, and a monkey wrench – none of which belonged to her. She sat back on her heels, confused. Then her heart softened as she realized Boris, Trần and/ or Enzo must have popped the "gifts" into her bag – like a teacher's apple.

They were such sweet boys. No, *really*.

She returned to her search and checked her hair. It was no good. The house keys were gone. *Again.* She knew Alana would be upset, for Alana was sure she'd found a sure-proof way for her mom to never lose her keys again: *this* keychain sounded an alarm whenever you whistled. *But I can't whistle,* Emma had confessed, and proved this was the case by pursing her lips and producing a pathetic *pfft.*

In a house two suburbs away, however, someone's father was whistling very loudly indeed. The kind of whistle that said *Wow* and *Gee whiz* and *What the* ..? all at once. And every time it happened, a toddler's tummy emitted the strangest noise: a kind of *beep, beep, beep,* like an alarm, muffled by the extra-absorbent nappy he wore. This prompted another *Wow-gee-whiz-what-the…*-whistle. This would have continued indefinitely had the toddler's mother not investigated why a nappy change was taking so long. She whisked the child to the local hospital's emergency room at once – providing further proof to health officials that toddlers will put anything they find in the sandpit into their mouths.

"Everybody has got a key to our house except you!" Alana later accused Emma, and Emma had not very convincingly replied, "Surely not!" while secretly wondering if it wasn't a little bit true.

CHAPTER 26

The Toy Truck arsonist strikes again

Emma handed Alana a postcard, but not before taking a look at the picture. The girl in the image had the most incredible green eyes, deep-set and filled with laughter and secrets. Her dark skin was the perfect foil for the colorful scarf framing her face, while in the background, small mounds of intense hues hinted at the freshness of the spices being sold at the marketplace.

"Looks like James is in Morocco again," she said. "I hope he'll be back in time for the Elvis convention (no, don't ask) photo-shoot next week." With any luck, Emma's head would look less like a football by then (perfectly normal for wisdom-teeth extraction, the dentist had assured her, although Emma wasn't convinced) so she could conduct the celebrity interviews at the charity event looking semi-human.

Chapter 26

Alana gave a squeal of delight and dropped the newspaper she was reading. "Oh, that's so beautiful," she breathed, gazing at the picture postcard. She looked up after reading the back. "He said he'd be back in time for The Big Game."

"He wrote you a postcard all the way from Morocco to tell you that?"

"No, we've been Skyping and exchanging photos. He's helping me with algebra and stuff," she explained.

Emma looked at her daughter in surprise.

"And he comes to soccer practice most weekends when he's free."

"Well, I'll be ..." Emma's gaze turned thoughtful. She gave her daughter a hug and then stepped back, as if looking at Alana properly for the first time. "He's a big part of your life too, isn't he? And here I was thinking I knew everything there was to know about that man."

"Uncle James has some interesting secrets, you know," Alana said mysteriously.

"Well, so have I," Emma grinned. "I know

exactly what to get you for your birthday this year, and it's something you really, really love."

Alana groaned. Unlike her friends, who looked forward to their birthdays, Alana dreaded hers. If her mom behaved like other parents and bought the latest "i"-whatever, she would have been more than happy, but Emma wasn't like other parents. She planned Spectacular Events to make her daughter feel Special. Unfortunately, her Big Ideas were always too ambitious and ended in disaster.

"Please, Mom. Don't make any trouble –" Alana began, but Emma, mishearing, kissed Alana on her head, and said with a smile, "It's no trouble at all."

Alana sighed and went back to the article in the newspaper. *Another* fire had broken out in a local school. And at the crime scene, the arsonist had left another toy truck ... She *really* had to do something about Flynn! *Tout de suite.* Immediately!

CHAPTER 27

Busted!

Alana forced the *clang* and *jangle* of the Hare Krishna religious songs to the back of her mind as she focused her binoculars. She was missing extra soccer practice for this – she really hoped her hunch was going to pay off. Alana was pleased with her choice of location. From up here in the Hare Krishna restaurant, she could clearly see the florist and church hall, where she had last lost Flynn. She checked her watch. If he was punctual, he should be turning up soon. Four o'clock came and went. At five minutes past he was still a no-show. Alana began to have some doubts. But then, at 4:08, she spotted the familiar hoodie, drawn up to protect the wearer's identity. "Gotcha," Alana murmured, and watched as Flynn looked around furtively before ducking into a side alley.

Alana raced down the stairs, pressing a donation into the hands of a bald-headed attendant, who shook his tambourine in thanks. By the time she was able to investigate the alley, however, there was nowhere to go and nothing to see. The alley was a dead end, and Alana was sure Flynn had not come out. She spun around, the fading light revealed nothing but the odd commuter rushing to escape winter's icy fingers. Alana resisted the childish urge to stamp her feet.

She drifted away from the florist, where Fate made a second appearance, this time as a busker who had set up to perform. The musician was short, and somewhat squashed-looking. Despite the cold, his head was bare, revealing grassy tufts that grew at random. With eyes closed, he hit the top of two metal trashcans with drumsticks, and every now and then, the side of an upside-down bin.

Bang. Bing. Bang. Bing. Boom. Boom. Boom.

It was a jarring sound – not at all musical or rhythmic. Instead of inviting an audience in, it drove people away, Alana included. Only someone like Emma would have dropped a coin into the busker's woolly hat. Emma was forever dropping coins into busker's hats and open guitar cases, or pressing it into the hands of people who were down on their luck.

But Fate wasn't in the mood for a cacophony that evening. Nor was an angry middle-aged woman in a black woollen cardigan, leotard, skirt and tights. She opened the heavy door of the church hall and stalked out, demanding that the busker to move away with irate flourishes and agitated hands. Alana watched the unfolding drama and then looked beyond her into the hall's dark, woody depths. Something snagged her attention. Not something. Some*one*. Someone who looked an awful lot like ... *Flynn Tucker!* Alana had to pinch herself, for there, in charcoal gray tights that showed off perfectly the tautness of his muscled thighs, was Flynn, stretching at the barre. Alana's mouth began catching flies. "Do you mind?" the woman asked, blocking Alana's view, nose high in the air. "This is a private class," she said, before closing the church hall door with an emphatic *thud*.

Bad Boy was a bun-head?

Okay, maybe not a bun-head, since he was a boy. Alana wondered briefly what male ballet dancers were called. In French, it would be *danseur*. At the Police Boys' Club, she imagined it would be "death-wish." No wonder he was keeping it quiet.

Faint strains of Beethoven (or was it Bach?) escaped through the cracks in the door as Alana drew nearer to listen. She pressed her ear to the cold wood. She could just make out the words: *arabesque en lair, chassé, fondue* ... Alana could almost see the curved lines of Flynn's body, the smooth glide of legs moving forward and back as he gave the appearance of melting.

Alana rubbed her chin as she considered her next move. It looked like Ballet Boy wasn't going anywhere, not for the next hour or so at least. She shouldered her backpack and headed for Café Newtown, which sat across the road, to grab a bite to eat and do some homework. She ate. She worked. She waited. At ten minutes past six, Flynn emerged from the church hall, blowing on his hands. He wore a thick jacket over the hoodie.

It bore the brunt of the wind, which had picked up since Alana had first set up camp. She let him walk a few steps before prodding him sharply in the back, just as he had done to her at the cooking demonstration months before.

"Busted," she said amiably.

Flynn swung around. "What are *you* doing here?"

"Freezing my butt off, to tell the truth. But then, the truth isn't something you'd know much about, is it?" Alana accused.

Flynn stared. Although he didn't know Alana very well, he knew enough to recognize The Look – like a mastiff clenching a bone.

"Fine. But if you're going to give me the third degree, let's go somewhere warm with food. I'm starving."

Two hamburgers and half a strawberry smoothie later, Flynn allowed himself a contented burp before sitting back. His soft, silver eyes had darkened to a bottomless gray, and they were wary.

Alana didn't waste any time. "You're obviously not the Toy Truck Arsonist," she stated, rather than asked. "You've got a legitimate excuse, so why not fess up?"

"If my brother found out I was doing ballet, he'd kill me. He's not exactly a fan of the arts, shall we say." Flynn's lips twisted into a grimace.

"So if *you* haven't been lighting the fires, then who *has*?"

"*Ce n'est pas mon secret à dire*," he muttered in French. "How should I know?" he denied in English with a shrug.

Alana's eyes narrowed. The cogs of her mind spun as she struggled with the translation. Bits of the puzzle clicked into place. "It's your brother, isn't it?"

"What? No. Where'd you get a stupid idea like that? Talk about random!"

"'Not my secret to tell,' you said, so I'm guessing it's your brother's."

Flynn was shocked. "You speak French?"

Alana forged on. "And I bet he's done this sort of thing before. Come on, spill the beans. I've got a computer-hacking genius and I'm not afraid to use him."

Flynn gave in. He could see that Alana wasn't going to let it go, and in a way it was a relief to tell someone. He'd been carrying the secret around for so long that he could feel its weight around his neck every time he breathed. "Alright. Yes. He's got a rap sheet as long as my arm. Daniel's been in and out of delinquents' programs and juvenile detention all his life. With this latest escapade, he would've been locked up for sure, so I wore it for him. Because I confessed, my last school agreed not to put it on my permanent record. Gibson High would only take me if I joined their rehabilitation program ..."

"...kickboxing," Alana added.

Flynn nodded. "Daniel promised he wouldn't do it anymore. Promised he'd stay clean. This move was supposed to be a fresh start." Flynn's lips twisted again, this time into a sad smile. "I should've known he'd lie."

"No offense, but why would you cover for such a jerk?"

"I don't expect you to understand. You're an only

child, right?" Alana nodded. "He's my brother," Flynn said simply. "He's all I've got. After Mom walked out ..." Flynn paused. There was silence. It crushed. It squeezed. "Even if he *is* a jerk, I'd do anything to protect my brother."

If Shakespeare had taught Alana anything that year, it was that although characters could be powerless against their fate, they at least had control over their reactions to it. Fate had handed Flynn a difficult choice.

But Fate had given one to Alana, too.

Alana looked into Flynn's eyes, which were now a stormy gray. She could keep quiet, but decided to dive into the waiting tempest. "You know what? I may not know much about having brothers and sisters, but I know this much. People do stuff like that, stupid stuff, sometimes because it's a cry for help. Any attention, even negative attention, is better than being ignored. I mean, why leave a toy truck at the crime scene unless a part of you wanted to get caught? But you're not going to stay under 18 forever." Alana let that sink in before continuing.

"Whatever you choose to do," Alana paused to look deeper into Flynn's eyes, "don't leave it too late. Don't let him screw up your life. If you turn him in, he'll know you did it for the right reason."

Flynn wiped his mouth with his sleeve and shrugged. Family was never easy. It didn't have a rule book or come with instructions. But things *were* getting more serious now. Maybe Alana was right. Maybe Daniel was crying out for help and, like it or not, he and his dad had to listen.

Alana got up to go. "By the way," she said, pausing at the door, "how come he leaves a toy truck?"

Flynn gave an embarrassed grin. "Daniel *Tucker*? It rhymes with *trucker*. Get it?"

A look of understanding entered Alana's eyes as she wrinkled her nose in distaste.

"Yeah, I know," Flynn conceded. "He's a jerk *and* a moron. But he's *my* jerk, *my* moron."

CHAPTER 28

The Big Game

Alana placed a big cross through the date on her calendar which she had circled in red months ago. The girls' soccer team had been training all season for this day, and Alana's heart was pounding. She tried to push her nerves aside as she balanced a ball on her ankle and flicked it into the air. The *pum, pum, pum* of it bouncing off her foot echoed down the stairs.

"What? What? Who is it?" Emma groaned muzzily from the doorway of her office.

Alana jumped the final few stairs and landed with a *thump* next to her mom.

"Big game today, Mom. Remember?" Alana said, half in reproach. Her mom had obviously forgotten about the soccer match ... *again*.

Emma peered through her bird-nest hair, lips working silently in concentration. "Ooh, ooh, The Big Game. Of course. I remember." Alana glared at the lie. "Well, okay, I didn't remember it was *today*, but I did know about it. I even invited Oliver. He said he liked sports, and I thought we could do brunch afterwards."

"So you're seeing him again?" Alana asked, automatically measuring out Emma's coffee into the *Atomic* coffeemaker and putting it on the stovetop. It wasn't long before the pungent aroma of ground beans filled the small kitchen. Harry-or-Leo paused mid-scurry to take an appreciative whiff before scuttling into the shadows.

Emma smiled weakly. "I'm not sure," she answered vaguely. "Brunch with you and your friends isn't really a date, is it?"

There was a knock at the door. Khalilah burst in, bouncing with excitement, as usual. Sofia followed her in, weighed down with more good luck charms than ever before. She could barely lift her head. The rest of the team was meeting them at the field.

"Breakfast, anyone?" Alana offered.

"Ooh, no, I feel too nervous to eat," Khalilah

said with a rueful rub of her stomach. "Maybe just a cheese toastie?"

"No food for me," Sofia said, equally anxious, "but I'd love a cup of tea."

The girls had their breakfast in silence, each submerged in her own thoughts. A crackling silence filled the kitchen. Alana held her soccer ball close in one arm like a security blanket while she ate a slice of toast. Khalilah made a second toastie for extra power, and Sofia tipped her cup upside-down to read the tea leaves.

"Either a hurricane is coming," she said, looking up with a worried frown, "or we're going to lose."

Khalilah looked thoughtful. "Yes, but where do we stand statistically?"

"*Statistically*, we're due for a win. But," Sofia gazed out at the cloudless sky, "it's not exactly hurricane weather."

Alana laughed. "Sydney doesn't get hurricanes, Sof. Come on. Think positive! Rub a Buddha belly or something."

While Sofia got rubbing, and Khalilah packed

a third toastie for the car, Emma returned with the news that James would give them a ride. Emma's car had still not recovered since the high-speed car chase.

Khalilah hung out of James's car window like an excited toddler, pointing out all the tourist spots along the way. "That's where I took my aunt and uncle," she said of Chinatown and, "We went there, too" as they passed Darling Harbor. By the time they were crossing the Sydney Harbor Bridge, Khalilah was beside herself. "We walked all the way to the top!" she said proudly. "My brother was so jealous, but Bapa said he would take him again when he comes."

This came as news to her friends.

"What? You didn't say your brother was coming!" Sofia exclaimed.

"When?" Alana asked, grateful for the diversion.

As Alana and Sofia pumped Khalilah for more information (Jefri was coming next year, after graduating from his religious studies), Emma flicked through the pile of CDs for some music to listen to. The cover of one of them caught Alana's eye.

"Ooh, please can we play that one, Uncle James?" Alana begged. A bit of hardcore rock would be just the thing to smash the butterflies that had invaded her stomach.

Emma looked at the cover dubiously. Three canines in various stages of decay were dressed in Tudor costume. The dogs were enclosed by an ornate, golden frame. James smiled at Emma and deftly exchanged the CD for another. "I think I'd much prefer to play *this* one."

Nyah, nyah, nyah, nyah, nyah (Drumsticks - One, two, three, four)

You think you can handle this?
Oh yeah ... I don't think so.
You think you're so hard to resist?
Oh yeah ... I don't think so.

Alana, Sofia and Khalilah grinned at each other. It was *their* song, "Stormy Heart" – the one that had won them the original song competition and tickets and backstage passes last year. The three girls jounced in the car seat as they sang along. Even James and Emma joined in the chorus. By the time they arrived at the oval, everyone was in a jubilant mood. Maybe the Soccer Academy *wasn't* going to win this year.

Alana and her friends tumbled out of the car to look for the rest of their team. Fans of the Soccer Academy's BlueJays were easily spotted, in their customary blue-and-green-striped scarves and jerseys. It looked like almost everybody was touting a *Go BlueJays!* flag or poster. The Gibson Gibbons' gear looked childish in comparison, with yellow squiggles on dirty gray T-shirts, because – as the school uniform designer had pointed out – they were bound to get dirty anyway. Alana spotted a handful of supporters from their school huddled close to the hotdog stand. Spring was just around the corner, but it was still nippy at 8:30 in the morning.

Khalilah jumped up and down. She always fidgeted when she was excited. Maddie, Prita, and Preyasi had joined them. The whole team was here now. "So, are you pumped?" Khalilah asked them.

"Bring it on," Alana and Maddie said together, and then burst out laughing.

Sofia handed good luck charms to each of the players: a strip of four-leaf clover fabric she tied around their heads *kamikaze*-style.

Maddie looked at it, puzzled. "How come this material looks familiar?"

Sofia shrugged casually, "That's because I cut up my lucky shorts."

"Eww, Sofia," Khalilah squealed, "You mean this used to rub against your butt?"

"Umm, girls," Prita interrupted. "I think we have more –"

"– important things to worry about," Preyasi finished.

The BlueJays team strode onto the field. Blue and green streaks of sunscreen slashed their cheeks, warrior-style. Each wore an expression of fierce concentration as they began their warm-up. From their footwork, they were a tight team. The next 45 minutes would not be easy.

Chapter 28

Sofia turned around and clapped her hands decisively. "Right. Okay. They don't look too bad. Let's warm up too, shall we? Stretch our muscles? The leg ones. And arm ones," she said, bending and lunging, and then twisting at the waist. The others followed suit and then began to practice with their own ball. They called a halt after ten minutes – the coach had arrived, but it was not who they were expecting.

"Coach *Kusmuk*? But where's Coach McNeeson?" Prita asked, clearly disappointed.

"Hamstring injury," she snapped. "That's a *leg* one," she aimed at Sofia with a sneer. "I don't expect you to get very far with today's competition, so let's get the humiliation over with. I've got better things to do with my Sunday than babysitting you," she said. "Let's go."

Sofia was loath to draw attention to herself, but had to protest. "Coach McNeeson usually gives us a pep talk before the game ..." she trailed off.

Coach Kusmuk sighed. "Fine. Try not to get yourselves killed. Okay, talk over. Let's go."

Friends and relatives of the team arrived with cameras and mobile phones to take a commemorative shot. Even with all the tricks James had up his sleeve as a professional photographer, the team's smile was strained and Coach Kusmuk's expression was filled with boredom.

The referee turned up and, with him, a different BlueJays team. The Gibbons turned to each other and the coach in bewilderment, as the team they'd been expecting to play walked off the field.

"Wha-?"

"Who?"

"That was the BlueJays Under-9s Team. You're playing the Soccer Academy's Under-13s B-side – the BlueJay Bruisers," Coach informed them with a familiar smirk.

Sofia gulped. "'*B*-side'?"

Maddie looked up at the towering Amazons. "Looks like some people hit puberty years ago."

CHAPTER 29

Gibbons vs. Bruisers

Emma knew little about the rules of soccer, and spent most of her time asking questions of James, and Sofia, who was in reserve.

"Are you sure that girl is allowed to do that?" she asked as one of the Bruisers shoved Alana out of the way and took off with the ball. Alana followed in hot pursuit.

"The Soccer Academy is certainly playing a rough game, but that's soccer," James shrugged, and then cringed as Maddie hit a wall of flying feet and flailing elbows.

"I don't think shin pads are enough protection. They look like they could do with full-body armor," Emma said faintly.

At which Alana landed at Emma and James's feet, squashed by a much bulkier girl, who used Alana's head as support to lever herself back up.

Emma crouched down until she could see

Alana at eye level. "Are you having fun, LaLa?" she asked in concern. James, meanwhile, yelled about "fouls" and being "offside," and when that didn't get results, began saying unkind things about the referee's mother.

Alana hoisted up her shorts and spat out a mouthful of grass. "Okay," she growled, "if *that's* how you want to play..."

What followed was a brutal game that was still locked at nil-nil at halftime. The teams headed for opposite sides of the field for a drink of water and a word from the trainers. The BlueJay Bruisers' coach, known around the circuit as Battle-Axe, was giving his team a severe tongue-lashing. At 135 centimeters high, he looked like a toddler having a tantrum.

"Unacceptable!" he squeaked, "What are you doing out there? You're running around like a bunch of hairdressers!" There was a long-standing rivalry between the Bruisers' and Gibbons' coaches. The competition between the two coaches went beyond the mere game of soccer.

It went further than the geography of the field. The pair had been fighting for years. The thought of one of his teams, *his teams*, being beaten by "Big Mac" McNeeson was unthinkable!

Coach Kusmuk turned around to face the Gibson Gibbons with something nearly resembling a smile. "Okay, you've survived the first half. Now it's crunch time. You've got a decent shot at winning, much more than I thought, so listen up, here's what I want you to do." The six girls formed a tight huddle while Coach Kusmuk rapidly explained the game plan.

The crowd took advantage of the ten-minute break to get in line for coffee. The sky had turned overcast. Weak sunlight struggled through the thick skein of cloud cover. Parents stamped their feet to generate more warmth and wrapped their hands around hot beverages, while young children pretended to be soccer heroes, dodging tackles, scoring goals, knees skidding in the dirt in triumph.

"Goal!" yelled Maddie's little brother, Troy,

arms thrust out in flight as he did a victory lap of the field. "Goal!" echoed Cassy not far behind.

James checked his camera's counter and grimaced. "I haven't got many shots of Alana playing. I always get too involved in the game."

Emma gave his arm a reassuring squeeze. "That doesn't matter. It means a lot to Alana you just being here. It means a lot to *me*. It's really special."

James looked at Emma's hand, which was still holding his arm. "She's a special girl," he whispered.

There was something about the way he said it which made Emma think he'd stopped talking about Alana.

Emma snatched her hand away. "Anyway," she said, nervously, "I'm sure Oliver is around here somewhere taking shots. He promised to bring his camera."

"Ah, yes. The Boyfriend," James muttered darkly.

There was a loud commotion and the crowd parted. What emerged was not a famous, book-writing Teen Expert as Emma expected, but two cart-wheeling cheerleaders in mini-skirts who definitely weren't from Gibson High – they were far too old for that. The onlookers looked bemused as the pair gave each other Rs, Is, Bs, Bs, Os, Ns and Ss and yelled, "Go Ribbons!" to nobody in particular.

"It's Gibbons, not Ribbons, you idiots," Emma admonished good-naturedly.

"Ribbons, Gibbons, same-same lah!" Ling Ling panted.

"Oh hi, James!" Katriona cried, spotting the photographer, who was doing his best to hide. She shook her pom-poms and wagged her bottom in what she thought was a cute manner. A pose was struck. Another of her favorites: bent leg, hand on hip, while the other lifted a pom-pom in victory. "Cheese," she said through clenched teeth.

James mumbled a hasty "gottagotakealeak" and rushed away.

Katriona watched his retreating back, looking miffed. "You know, there's something funny about that guy."

"Who? James?" Emma asked with half an ear as she continued to scan the crowd for Oliver.

"Uh-huh," Katriona said with narrowed eyes. "I think he's, *you know*."

"Who? *James*?" Emma repeated, this time her attention caught like a fly snagged in honey.

"Yep," Katriona said confidently.

"Oh no," Emma said, rejecting the idea instantly. Hadn't they just had A Moment, with her holding his arm and him talking about a Special Girl?

"Maybe ..." Ling Ling considered the idea.

"Definitely," Katriona said. "Otherwise," she asked, running a hand up and down the length of her body, "why would he be running away from all of *this*?"

The shrill call of the referee's whistle snatched their attention from answering as the players resumed their game.

"Go Gibbons!" Emma called out, clapping. Katriona and Ling Ling attempted star jumps and landed on their knees. There was a sympathetic "*Ow!*" from the crowd.

As the team applied Coach Kusmuk's strategy, the game began to look like a strange fusion of soccer, gymnastics and obstacle course training. Preyasi stole possession from one of the Bruisers with an inside-cut and passed it swiftly to her twin, Prita, who was waiting for the ball. Prita dodged the Bruisers' offensive – two beefy girls who came charging – with some adroit footwork that looked like the tiptoe-through-tires-exercise. At the last minute she passed the ball back to Preyasi, who drove it halfway down the field. Alana picked up the ball mid-flight with a cartwheel that ended in a scissor kick aimed at Maddie, who headed for goal. It bounced off the post with a *dong!* There was a groan of disappointment from Gibbons' supporters. Within moments of the goal kick, the Gibbons had repossession of the ball and passed it backward, forward, and sideways – always keeping the ball away from the Bruisers with their adept maneuverings. There was no doubt that the obstacle training had improved the Gibbons' fitness and stamina. In this second half the bigger girls were being run ragged.

When the Gibbons' second goal attempt missed, the BlueJay Bruisers' coach exploded. "Don't you dare stop," he screamed at the top of his voice, "You don't stop until one of you has a heart attack!" His team limped back into position. The BlueJay goalie, having stopped the ball with her stomach, looked like she wanted to throw up. One of them coughed up a tooth. Another looked like she'd twisted an ankle. "Strap it. Cut it off. I don't care," the BlueJay coach yelled, "just don't come off that field without a win."

Coach Kusmuk had only one command: "You know what you have to do. Go do it."

Kusmuk's strategy was simple: keep possession of the ball and make the other team do all the running. Their opponents found that whenever they tackled, the ball mysteriously disappeared elsewhere. Running in circles was getting the Bruisers nowhere. "Where are you going?" their coach kept yelling. "Don't go all National

Geographic on me!" Out of sheer frustration, one of their strikers charged, even *after* Maddie no longer had the ball. After a body-slam, she drove a vicious kick into Maddie's shin that left her lying on the field, curled up in a tight ball of pain.

"Foul!"

"Yellow card!"

"Red card!"

"Free kick!" spectators cried.

Maddie's family and the Gibson Gibbons ran over to Maddie, but were helpless. There was nothing for it but to take her off the field. It was unlikely she would return. Coach Kusmuk turned to Sofia and looked her up and down – from her purple-dyed hair, tied back with her lucky shorts, to the shamrock-patterned knee-highs she sported. "I guess you're in." The look she gave was not encouraging.

The clock ticked. The score remained nil-all. Battle-Axe was beside himself with alarm as he hopped up and down on the sidelines.

"What's with the leprechaun?" a voice said beside Emma.

"Oliver!" she cried. "You made it!" She held out her hand for a handshake while he bent to kiss her cheek. Then she went to kiss his cheek as he held out his hand for a handshake. They settled for an awkward wave at each other. "I think Alana's just about to do something."

"You're just in time. Alana's taking a free kick. Hi, I'm James," James said, interrupting and extending a hand (was he standing straighter?) toward the much-taller Oliver.

"Good to meet you, James," Oliver said in turn (was his voice suddenly deeper?) "I'm Dr. Gray, but please call me Oliver."

The two men gripped hands in a handshake that was too firm and lasted too long. In cavemen's times they would have reached for clubs.

The referee called Alana to take the free kick. Alana took a deep breath to calm down. Five girls stood between her and the goal. Five girls stood between her team and a shot at winning.

"Lana! Lana! Lana!" the supporters chanted. "Piranha!" a quieter voice could be heard.

Three minutes. Too low, and the Bruisers would be able to block it. Two minutes. Too high, and it would miss the goal altogether. Sixty seconds. Too soft, and the goalie would be able to stop it in its tracks. Forty. A sudden hush fell on the crowd as the realization dawned: a Soccer Academy team had *never* been defeated. Twenty. *Was this about to change?* Ten, nine, eight, seven, six.

Alana looked over at Maddie who smiled back through clenched teeth. Someone had found a bag of ice for her leg but she was still in a lot of pain. The sight of her friend's bravery filled Alana with a sudden volcanic fury. "This one's for you, Maddie," she breathed as her foot connected with the ball. The goalkeeper stretched her body and leapt high into the air to her right, every muscle taut and straining. The ball flew – it was like trying to catch a shooting star – and skimmed over the goalkeeper's gloves into the net! Goal! There was a long, shocked silence. As if remembering himself, the referee sounded the whistle, ending the game.

Alana was immediately surrounded by teammates and supporters, who lifted her on their shoulders and yelled and screamed wildly. She cast around for her mom, who was grinning broadly, and then for James, who was trying not to cry. Maddie was pumping her fist into the air as Troy and Cassy did a victory lap around her.

Emma turned to Oliver in excitement and stopped. Oliver had his shirt off. Again. This time he was showing Katriona and Ling Ling his "dancing pecs." The two cheerleaders had started a new chant. "Give me a 'P'!" "'P'!" they screamed. Finally, the Gibbons' victory penetrated the trio's cocoon.

Oliver looked up. "We won?"

"Yes," Alana said, unimpressed by his display. "*We* did."

"Well, let's go to Calorie King to celebrate!" Oliver suggested.

"Nitro-ices, my treat!" James said at the same time.

Chapter 29

"How about a *Hi-5* concert?"

"IMAX theater, anyone?" they said simultaneously, again.

The two men exchanged a look of frustration. Oliver bowed, as if to say, "after you," to which James responded with a, "no, no, no, after you" bow of his own.

"Well, who wants to drive in a classic 780 Coupe Volvo with full leather interior and off-road suspension?" Oliver said confidently. "And if you say please, I'll keep my shirt off," he added in a loud whisper to Katriona and Ling Ling, who giggled.

James just smiled and shrugged. *How can I compete with that?* his twisted grin seemed to say.

Alana and her friends exchanged a look. A boxy Volvo, dancing pecs, Golden Oldies music (probably), a diet fast-food chain and then a kiddies' concert, *OR* a Mini Cooper, a guy who keeps his shirt on, *Dead Dogs Rotting* blaring on the speakers, ice cream made with liquid nitrogen, and larger-than-life heroes in 3D …

It was no contest.

Katriona and Ling Ling linked arms with Oliver and followed him, stumbling, across the field. Both of them had abandoned sunglasses for sleeping masks – determined to give the skin around their eyes maximum protection from the sun.

Oliver stopped and turned. "Coming, Emma?" he asked.

Emma looked at James, whose expression was unreadable. She turned to Oliver. "Yes." *I suppose,* she added to herself.

Alana tried hard to ignore the prickle of warning that always preceded a premonition that something was Terribly Wrong. For a "teen expert," Dr. Oliver Gray was drastically out of touch with what her and her friends were into. He didn't ride the Harley that he was supposed to own. And after the heart-to-heart Emma had shared with Alana and her friends the other night, it was clear he knew more about tooth decay than any normal person *should.* But the Bruisers' coach came marching over before she could connect the dots.

"Not bad, girlies, not bad. But keep in mind that the Bruisers are the Blue-Jays' *B*-Team. You may have defeated *them,* but the Blue-Jay Barbarians are on a whole other level." He looked them up and down, and, satisfied with what he saw, laughed. "See you next year then, eh? And please, give my heartfelt congratulations to McNeeson, won't you?" he added insincerely, handing over some official paperwork. "Pass that on to the Gibbons' coach, there's a good lad," he said to a shocked Kusmuk.

The team tried very hard not to meet Coach Kusmuk's furious expression when the tiny man left. They almost succeeded in melting away into the crowd too, but the coach was not letting them off so easily.

"I hope you enjoyed today's warm-up, everyone. Tomorrow's obstacle training will teach you to push through the pain barrier," she promised. "You'll need the extra help if you're to compete against the Barbarians."

The team groaned. They didn't really want that kind of help. Hearts sank and muscles ached at the thought.

"Tomorrow?" Khalilah whimpered. "Kill me *now.*"

CHAPTER 30
A second, second chance

The inner suburbs of Sydney used to have a large number of working warehouses, but with the shift of something called Global Economics, many were converted into high-priced residences, shop-houses, and in the case of Gibson High, schools. In one such abandoned warehouse, with the roof half-gone and the brick-work still in piles of rubble, Emma's latest project with the Second-Chancers was thriving. Literally.

The idea came to her as she was puttering in the garden. Impressed, as always, by nature's ability to thrive and grow in the face of adversity – neglect, over-watering, misread instructions for fertilizer – Emma daydreamed about Dr. Gray's latest advice from his book: *"To nurture something successfully is to know a huge sense of achievement."* She watched the spray of the hose arc its way over the leaves, darkening the soil beneath. Once she'd thought of it, the idea seemed to grow with as much speed and enthusiasm as the noxious weeds she cultivated. Nurturing a plant was something Emma was confident the Second-Chancers could do. After all, if she could do it, anyone could. So she negotiated the temporary use of a warehouse and surrounding grounds. Visions of towering sunflowers, sun-kissed organic tomatoes, and leafy jungle palms crowded an already over-productive imagination. Within weeks, the reality was even more breathtaking than Emma had hoped.

Tall plants reached for the ceiling with impossibly healthy leaves, green and luscious. The air in the renovated greenhouse reminded Emma of thick syrup, sweet and heavy. The scent of fertile soil was intoxicating. It was the smell, Emma told the group of nervous teenagers, of Success.

At this announcement, Enzo let out a sigh of relief.

"You see. I told you she be cool," a cocky Trần told him.

"Cool?" Emma cried. "I'm more than cool. I'm

so proud of you guys. It's amazing." She made a sweeping gesture with her arm at all the plants. "Look at what you've achieved!"

"We were worried you might not, you know, approve of them," Boris whispered. "You know ... because it's weeds."

Emma threw her hands up in the air and laughed. "Oh, I think you'll be surprised to know I've got an even BIGGER stack of weeds in my own garden," she said.

Enzo beamed and dug at the ground with hands as big as shovels. He unearthed a plant and placed it with infinite care into a pot. He handed it to Emma shyly. Emma felt a lump in her throat. She was bursting with pride and happiness.

Outside the warehouse grounds, ex-traffic officer, PC Henley, crouched behind a shed. *This is what I'm talking about*, he said to himself. *THIS is living.* Henley's heart pounded in his ears and he felt breathless. He took out his inhaler and administered two swift puffs. He spoke rapidly into a walkie-talkie.

The walkie-talkie in his hand crackled and popped, thick with interference. "Krrssh ... -orry ... could you ... -peat that, over?"

"I said we are good to go. Operation Stink-Bomb is good to go and we are going in. Hold your positions."

"Sorry, Sarge, but I think my battery's dead," a voice said next to him, making Officer Henley jump and squeal.

"I told you to hold your positions," he hissed. "Oh, never mind. Stay here while we move in. Stealth and silence from here on, everyone," Henley ordered his crew. He put on a helmet of marigolds and ferns and crept forward after a series of complicated hand signals. With a sigh, the rest of the police officers donned a floral disguise and followed. Four flowerpots glided in.

"Right, everyone! Hands up! This is the police," Officer Henley yelled, brandishing a gun, the barrel of which was somehow sprouting a daisy.

It is said that the mind sees what it wants to see and the ears hear what they want to hear. Caught as she was in the heat of the moment, and with a love for all of humanity threatening to split open her heart, Emma didn't see a Law Enforcement Officer but a Flower Power Soul Mate. "Make love, not war!" she cried, as she clutched her new potted plant in one arm and hugged Officer Henley with the other.

"*You*?!" Officer Henley squealed in recognition before making the arrest with hands that trembled. He jumped back a safe distance just in case.

Hours later, Judge Debnham sighed, shook her head, and tutted as she read the report. Every now and then the words "Communication Skills," "Team-Building," and "Nurture Nature Project" were thrown into the air like clay pigeons and shot down with snorts of disbelief and disgust. Frustration rolled off her back like waves. Emma looked at the clock on the wall for the seventeenth time.

"I hope I'm not keeping you," Judge Debnham said sweetly, breaking into Emma's jumbled thoughts.

"Oh no, not at all," Emma said with a nervous smile, which died the moment she looked into the steely eyes of the magistrate.

"Good, because I am only going to say this once, so you had better listen very closely. In the interests of society I hereby absolve you of any further community hours with the Second-Chancers of the Newtown Police Boys' Club and," her eyes bored into Emma's, "if I hear of you going anywhere near them, I shall put a restraining order on you. Is that clear?"

"I, I don't understand, Your Highness ... I think I'm making real progress," Emma protested.

"No doubt you are, but not in the direction this court intended," Judge Debnham intoned. "Stay away, Ms. Oakley, and KEEP away." Before she banged her gavel to dismiss her, the judge gave Emma a piercing look that pinned her to her chair. "I'm also very curious about these items we found in your handbag." She retrieved a flashlight, a butane torch, and a monkey wrench – presents from one or all of the Second-Chancers – from

Emma's favorite handbag, and then her Mexican *sombrero* (packed in readiness for another "ride" on the Harley), a crowbar, a mask and a rubber chicken. Each item was placed on the court's bench for display.

The *ding! ding! ding!* from a mobile phone shattered the leaden silence. The ringtone was a jaunty jingle that promised soda. Hugo! Somebody in the courtroom had Hugo's jingle as their ringtone, Emma realized, amazed. What a coincidence! She had only heard it as a ringtone once before...

The judge snapped at the bailiff, who rushed to confiscate the offending device. Emma turned to see who it belonged to. A weedy figure in a baggy leather jacket handed over his phone. Their eyes met. The expression in them changed as realization dawned. You! They both seemed to say.

Emma's mind spun as it made a series of mental connections. She was transported back in time. Back to a shivery night in Darlinghurst when she'd almost been tattooed with a cute little bunny rabbit with fierce teeth. Back to a time when she'd translated a robber's intentions to a shopkeeper who couldn't understand English. A robber who had threatened them all with a rubber chicken...

Hugo's jingle. Robbery. *Rubber chicken.*

Judge Debnham read out the message on the phone. "It appears your mother would like a box of tampons, young man," she informed him with relish. "The..."

"...silky, cotton kind," Emma said to herself in a daze. How could she not have realized it before? Well, he *had* been wearing a mask, she conceded. But why hadn't he recognized *her*? Then Emma remembered she had been wearing that ridiculous Mexican *sombrero* and the robber a mask, the corner shop *had* been poorly lit, and maybe all Asians *did* look alike...

The "*waaah*!" of the rubber chicken broke through Emma's thoughts. "I repeat, Ms Oakley. Do enlighten me about these curious items in your handbag."

Chapter 30

Emma exchanged a look with the youth and then turned to the judge. "I'm doing some improvements at my home, Your Honoress," she forced a smile, "I'm the kind of person who likes to … *fix* things," she said with a pointed look behind her. The youth appeared to squirm. Emma turned back and said sweetly, "I'm happy to help out at *your* home, if you want."

The judge looked at her keenly. She drummed her neatly manicured fingernails on the bench. She looked at the mobile phone, the boy (who was holding his breath) and, lastly, the rubber chicken, which hung limply in her other hand. "Thank you, but if I catch you anywhere near my home, Ms. Oakley, rest assured you will be arrested for trespassing." Then Judge Debnham was struck by another thought, and motioned for the bailiff to bring Emma's bag for reinspection. "Ah ha!" she exclaimed in victory, shaking a small plastic container of painkillers like a guilty maraca. "Have you seen to that tooth of yours yet?" She leaned forward in suspicion.

Emma, relieved at last to tellthetruththe wholetruthandnothingbutthetruthsohelpherGod, pitched forward and opened her mouth as wide as she could to display four gaping holes.

Judge Debnham recoiled. "Thank you. That will be all. Good day," she said, banging her gavel at last.

...

Judge Debnham had been more than clear – *Stay away, Ms. Oakley, and KEEP away* – which was why, outside the courtroom, Emma was giving a stone pillar a Good Talking To. "'Teacher's apple' my eye! That's it! No more robberies! No more, 'Stick'emupgivemeallyourmoney' crud," she fumed.

"But Miss," a nearby voice protested as it addressed a massive shrub, "you said, 'No swearing.'" "I said no swearing from YOU, and *stop* trying to change the subject. You need to work out what your gift is in life and start using it for the benefit of others, because deep down you *are* good, and you *are* smart, and you *can* do better." Emma said passionately. "I *believe* in you," she told the impassive rock.

Office workers enjoying their lunch on the courthouse steps shuffled away from Emma and the boy. Talking to the shrubbery or stone pillars might be contagious.

The silence was interrupted by a sniffle. The tiniest kind. It was a sniffle trying very hard to be snuffed. Nobody had EVER told him he was good. Nobody had ever called him smart. Nobody, much less himself, thought he could do better. Emma *believed* in him? *Him*?

He squared his shoulders and stood up straighter. "Okay, I'll try," he told the leafy bush thickly. "And Miss Emma?"

"Yes?"

There was a damp snuffle and a smear, like a glistening snail trail, as the leather jacket's sleeve was used as a tissue.

"Thanks... for everything."

"You're welcome." Emma wiped away a small tear of her own. "And please... say goodbye to the others for me."

"Sure."

Emma waited until the footsteps had died away before turning. She could just make out the writing on the back of the leather jacket, which replaced the original embroidery. "The Imbécile," it now read. "Good luck, Boris," she whispered.

CHAPTER 31

A blindfold. A birthday.
And a BIG boo-boo.

Alana prepared for her fourteenth birthday with care. Unlike other girls her age who agonized over which clothes to wear and what hairstyle to choose, Alana's preparations included updating her first aid kit, reading a compendium of anti-venoms, and completing a refresher course in CPR. Not that she knew where she was celebrating her birthday yet. All she'd been told was to dress in comfortable sports gear. Alana threw on a *Dead Dogs Rotting* T-shirt and faded, gray-spotted shorts.

Emma's smile slipped only for a moment when she saw Alana in the explicit T-shirt. "You look ... nice, Alana."

"Yes. Your outfit goes perfectly with the blindfold we've brought," Ling Ling enthused.

"Blindfold?" Alana protested, turning to face

her mom. "What do I need a blindfold for?" Her mind raced. *What next? A firing squad?*

"Oh, sweetheart," Emma said, "relax. If you knew where we were going, you'd guess right away. You know how I like to surprise you."

"You got that right," Alana muttered.

"Nevermind, Lana, we've got your back," Khalilah said with a wink. After seeing her friend's photo album, she knew what a fiasco Alana's birthday was each year and understood Alana's trepidation.

"Yes, now open your presents before we go," Sofia squealed excitedly. "This one's from the three of us." Sofia held out a small, thick package which Alana shook and rattled close to her ear.

"Hmm, it's a bit big for a good luck charm," she teased as she tore the paper. "Oh," she gasped, "thanks, you guys," holding up a set of Shakespeare graphic novels, a new guitar pick, and a T-shirt with the word: "Hardcore" written in bold below a picture of a half-eaten apple.

"They're awesome." She gave each of her friends a quick hug. "I'll wear it now." Emma threw Alana's friends a grateful glance as she watched the rotting dogs disappear beneath the new T-shirt.

Ling Ling pushed forward a large, heavy box which, Katriona muttered, was from them. Alana handled it as if it had the potential to explode. Never be deceived by packages wrapped up in pink butterflies and curly hearts. The paper was difficult to tear, but when she did finally get through, Alana was very surprised by what was there. Inside was a pair of boots with their own personality and attitude. They clearly said *"STOMP!"* in capitals and an exclamation mark at the end.

"You wear *those* for soccer and nobody's gonna mess with you," Ling Ling declared confidently.

Alana was touched. There was no way she would be allowed to wear the boots on the field, but no reason she couldn't wear them to school. As Ling Ling had said, nobody would dare mess with her if she did. Road-rage drivers included.

"Wah, I such a stylo milo one!" Alana said with a wink at Ling Ling, who gave her a *darn right* high five in return.

"Now it's my turn! Time for your blindfold," Emma sang, dangling a piece of polka-dot fabric. "We're meeting James at the... *oops*, almost let it slip," she giggled. "Come on. I don't want to be late."

Alana succumbed to the blindfold with great reluctance. The girls tittered with excitement in the background. They had no idea where they were going either. As soon as the car started, Alana tried very hard to figure out their destination by what she could hear and smell. She heard planes flying overhead and smelled the distinctive aromas of South King Street's exotic restaurants. From the stops and starts, she guessed they were traveling the length of King Street in traffic. She felt the car turn a corner after the railway station, after feeling a train's distinctive rumble through the bones of the battered car. If Alana's deductions were correct, they were heading for Gibson High. But why would her mom think going to school could possibly be a fun place for a birthday?! The car came to a shuddering stop. Alana's friends had gone strangely quiet. It was not a good sign.

"We're here!" Emma announced brightly. She guided Alana out of the car.

Judging from the sounds – basketball, swearing, the *clang* of a hoop – Alana's fear reached a new level. They walked forward and through a door. The sounds got louder and a foul aroma assaulted her nostrils. This wasn't school. It sounded and smelled like the Police Boys' Club!

"*Da-dah*!" Emma whipped off Alana's blindfold. Alana was right. She *was* in the Police Boys' Club. Why did her mom bring her here? The answer was right behind her. Just when she thought her fourteenth birthday couldn't get any worse, Maddie prodded her urgently.

Alana swung around. She looked, first at her mom and then up at Coach Kusmuk, who was in the kickboxing ring, warming up with roundhouse kicks and vicious jabs in the air. Nurse Cathy, who had volunteered to be on stand-by, stood beaming next to James, who was waving his camera.

"Between you and me," Emma confided to Alana, "I think Coach Kusmuk has forgotten all about that little boo-boo with my yo-yo."

As Alana gazed into Coach Kusmuk's eyes, which were like cold, hard chips of steel, she had to disagree. Apparently it had taken Coach Kusmuk *six weeks* to restore the contents of the Confiscation Cupboard after Emma's "little boo-boo."

"Mom —" she began, but Emma stopped her short and squeezed her hand.

"I know. You don't have to say it. You're welcome."

The lie she had told her mom months before poked out its tongue and blew a raspberry. *Interested? I love kickboxing! It's the most exciting sport ever.* Not.

Ding! Ding! Ding! A bell sounded. Nurse Cathy was so excited she began pacing. The pads of a defibrillator hung on her back like rectangular skillets. Alana couldn't help but notice that the nurse's arms were twisted and confined by a new fluffy, white sweater – a present from Mrs. Snell ("Not sure Mrs. Snell followed the knitting pattern properly," the nurse had confessed to colleagues in hushed overtones) – and as a result, Nurse Cathy looked like a contortionist with her head on backwards. Contrary to what Nurse Cathy thought, Mrs. Snell had been very pleased with the finished *straitjacket*. The design was perfect!

Alana felt as if she was in a dream as Sofia and Maddie tied the laces of the massive boxing gloves, which secured her hands in a heavy cocoon. Khalilah massaged her shoulders. Alana sat blankly in the corner. "It's Coach Kusmuk. It's Coach Kusmuk. It's Coach Kusmuk," she muttered. "It's Coach Kusmuk!" Her eyes grabbed Maddie's as reality finally sunk in.

"You can do this, Alana," Khalilah said urgently, peering down at her from upside down.

Sofia took off all of the good luck charms

around her neck and placed them over Alana's head. Alana's shoulders dropped. They weighed a ton!

Maddie scooped them all off again and handed them back. She then grabbed Alana's chin so they were forced to look into each other's eyes. Maddie's cousins did kickboxing, and they had taught her a few moves for fun. Maddie noted with a quick glance over her shoulder that Coach Kusmuk didn't look like she was here for fun, though. She looked like she was here to even the score. If Alana was going to come out of the ring alive, Maddie had to teach her some moves. Fast.

"Your basic punches are your jab – punching straight from the front hand – usually followed by a cross – which comes from one side of the body and finishes at the other. Next is your hook –"

"My hook," Alana echoed blankly.

"Yes. Your hook is a rounded punch which is thrown in an arc. Like this," Maddie said, demonstrating.

"Thrown in an arc," Alana repeated.

Chapter 31

"And the last punch..."

"...is the uppercut, which starts here," Flynn said, taking over from Maddie and pointing to Alana's belly, "and goes up toward Coach Kusmuk's chin."

"Coach Kusmuk!" Alana's eyes popped. "It's Coach Kusmuk. It's Coach Kusmuk. It's Coach Kusmu-" She had not even registered that Flynn was here... and that he was holding her hand...

Khalilah threw a glass of water in Alana's face with too much enthusiasm and was rewarded with a yell. Alana shook her head and tried to refocus on Flynn, who was describing roundhouse kicks, front-heel kicks, front kicks, side kicks, rising-knee strikes, and hooking-knee strikes.

Ding! Ding! Ding! The bell sounded again.

Coach Kusmuk gestured impatiently for Alana to enter the ring. She stumbled forward in a daze. The coach's slight form danced around Alana like she'd drunk too many cups of coffee. She demonstrated a few of her moves. A hook here. A kick there. Alana dodged the blows. Just.

"Come on, Oakley," the blur that was Coach Kusmuk taunted, "give it your best shot."

In the background, Alana was vaguely aware of raised voices: "*Two of you*?!" – then the murmur of an apology, but it was all Alana could do to avoid getting hit. That last swing had scraped her chin. Both of her T-shirts were drenched in sweat. She did her best to copy the figure in front of her, but was all too aware what a pathetic shadow she made – like a jerky puppet in slow motion. There was more shouting. This time about dentists and deception, double-crossings, and dancing pecs. Alana couldn't afford to get distracted but she couldn't help it.

Emma rubbed her eyes as she saw double. "So you're not Dr. Gray," she said to Oliver.

"I am. Just not *this* Dr. Gray," said not-Oliver-but-Donald sheepishly, pointing a thumb at his mirror image, who appeared just as confused as Emma. The *real* Dr. Oliver Gray was leaning against the Harley Davidson he had just wheeled out of the Second-Chancers' room. But for the pierced eyebrow and tattoo (not the wash-off kind), the two men were identical. *Identical twins.*

An extraordinary story unfurled. A story which contained two brothers. Oliver and Donald, were both doctors but in different fields. Donald confessed he'd decided to impersonate his brother and live his life because of Emma.

Oh, great, so it's my fault?

"Remember when I dropped in to visit Oliver? While he was on sabbatical? You were in his office reading his 'critically-acclaimed, award-winning' book," Donald said, rolling his eyes. "I met you and fell for you, but then I overheard you say you didn't want to go out with a dentist. I had no choice but to pretend to be him," he explained, chucking a thumb at his brother.

Of course, Alana thought to herself, it was so obvious! How could she have missed the signs? It explained why Donald couldn't ride the Harley, was so knowledgeable about teeth, and had absolutely no idea how to relate to her or her friends. Weren't Prita and Preyasi from the Gibson Gibbons impossible to tell apart? Dr. Donald Gray wasn't suffering from a split personality. He wasn't on drugs. He was a *twin*.

"So you're not an author, you're a dentist."

"Yes," Donald said.

"And the other guy in the operating theater...?"

"... is my partner. We share the dental practice."

"But *you* operated on me."

"Yes," Donald tried hard to look sheepish, but failed. "And look at what a great job I did! You *say* you don't want to go out with a dentist," Donald was saying, looking around for approval, "but you see, you really *do*."

Alana could have kicked herself for not figuring the mystery out sooner, but Coach Kusmuk was doing a pretty good job of that, on her own. Alana dragged her attention back to the action in the ring. Flynn was saying something to her.

"Come on, Alana," he urged. "You have to fight

smarter than that."

Alana's eyes were squeezed shut and she was jabbing blindly at the air. She felt a sharp slap on the back of her head. "Is that all you've got, Oakley?" the coach taunted. Alana tried hard to remember. *Roundhouse kicks, front-heel kicks, front kicks, side kicks, rising-knee strikes, hooking-knee strikes*, she repeated Flynn's advice to herself. Alana closed her eyes again and swung her leg around behind her in a powerful arc. Her foot connected with a *crack*. When she opened them, Coach Kusmuk was on the floor. Out cold. *C'est terrible*. This was another birthday fiasco she was sure to pay for once Coach Kusmuk woke up.

Nurse Cathy fought through the ring of students who had crowded around. "Right, somebody plug me in," she said, as Flynn undid the tie at Nurse Cathy's back.

"No, I really don't," Emma was telling Dr. Gray and rubbing a fist which was now quite sore.

On the floor of the Police Boys' Club,

somebody else was out cold.

Donald.

"You see," Sofia said with satisfaction as she surveyed the pair of lifeless bodies, "*I told you* there'd be a hurricane."

The End.

But what about Flynn... and his brother, Daniel... and... is there a Happy Ending???

Okayokayokay.

So, Flynn …

Flynn's father – Major Tucker – was Making An Effort, which was not easy because Tucker's Law had ruled the Tucker household for as long as any of them could remember. But a fire had been lit under his bum, so to speak, and now he was All Ears.

It was a lot to take in.

It was like a flood.

A flood of words.

His elder son wanted one of those Perfect Dads on TV that played with the kids and had poster-white teeth, and he wanted him to talk less and listen more, and would it kill him to *ask* every now and then rather than order? And while he was at it, he wanted him to take off that thick overcoat he never took off. *What coat?* The one that didn't let feelings in. Or out. The one he had put on after their mom walked out. And didn't come back. *Oh... That one.*

So with an arm around Daniel – tentative at first, because this was all new to him, and he would much rather demand his son drop down and give him twenty – Major Tucker glanced over at his younger son, who was grinning and crying at the same time. A *waterfall smile*, he would have said if he'd had the words.

"And you," he said instead, "you want to go dancing around in a tutu?"

"Yes, please," said Flynn.

EPILOGUE

The rich interior of the theater – red velvet curtains and golden filigree fretwork – glowed in the warm, pre-performance lights. The stage was set for the end-of-year Dance Showcase for the Pettigrew School of Dance. Near the front of the stage, two people were already seated: a man and his son. The older man, in crisp army fatigues, sat upright like a coiled wire of energy. The large youth next to him shifted uncomfortably. A warning bell sounded. People made their way to their seats, shuffling past and apologizing as they knocked knees with patrons already seated.

Four girls had to get past the man and his son to reach their seats. The first girl had long, purple dreadlocks past her waist, the curliest lashes and a wide smile. Layers of jewelery made her jangle as she walked. The large youth gazed after the trail of her long, flowing skirt. The second girl was lean, with long wavy hair and eyes like the ocean on a summer's day. The boy felt a sudden urge to go swimming. The third girl squeezed past with a shy giggle, and he had to fight the impulse to share the joke. She ducked her head into the interior of her hoodie and whispered to her friend, who laughed melodically. Her friend, the last girl to go past, had dark, wavy hair with a streak of rebellious plum and adorable dimples, he thought admiringly, until he looked into her eyes, which were as hard as stone. He dropped his gaze as if he'd been shot. The girls' conversation drifted over and, without knowing why, sucked him in.

"I can't wait to see him perform," said Dreads. "Is he any good?"

"Of course he's good," Giggles said with confidence. "He's good at everything."

"You're the only one who's seen him," Ocean Eyes said to Dimples – who had been invited, under the flag of *Truce*, to watch him rehearse. "What's he really like?"

Dimples shrugged and then admitted grudgingly, "I hate to say it, but he *is* amazing."

Giggles gave a squeal of delight while Dreads

groaned. "I still can't believe it. He's like the perfect guy – athletic, he can dance –"

"– he can cook – " Giggles added.

"– he plays sax – " Ocean Eyes sighed.

"– and he's loyal – " Dimples said with a quick glance at the boy next to her, who was hanging on their every word.

The boy couldn't resist the impulse to interrupt. "Sorry," he said, "but you can't mean to say you think ballet boys are ..." he pointed to the stage with a disbelieving snort.

"Hot."

"Wicked."

"The ultimate."

"But definitely..." said Dreads.

"...in the Friend Zone!" Ocean Eyes and Giggles sighed.

"Yep," admitted Dreads with a shudder, "kissing him would be like kissing one of my brothers."

"*Eww*," two of the girls squealed in sympathy. They felt exactly the same way. The boy took a closer look at the fourth girl and took in her *Dead*

Dogs Rotting T-shirt, black tutu, ripped tights and Seriously Studded Boots. She met his gaze steadily. Fate was here again, and she was quick to grasp the opportunity.

"Somebody once said that a man must be big enough to admit his mistakes, smart enough to profit from them, and strong enough to correct them. A *real man,* in other words, doesn't have to hide behind a kid brother," she said in a quiet voice, quickly placing a heavy boot over his shoe as he made to move away. "And if he looks good in a pair of tights, well," she said, so only he could hear, "even better."

The boy squirmed and looked down at his hands. Hands that had played with fire – and Dimples seemed to know it. "Do girls really think guys are hot, doing all that prancing and stuff?" he asked her.

Dimples looked at the boy – a larger, beefier, ill-tempered version of his brother – his father, and then at her friends, riveted in their seats, as Flynn took a flying leap into the future.

"What's hot," she said with a sudden realization, "is someone who loves so deeply that they'd do anything for the ones they love."

The End.

Really.

BIOGRAPHY

Poppy Inkwell writes a lot of different things.

Stories...

Website content...

Mandalas...

But not Christmas cards ... or not very often.

When she's not at her desk writing, you will find her ferreting in car boot sales, experimenting with food gastronomy, or playing with her camera.

Born in the Philippines, she now lives by the beach in Australia with one husband, two of her children, and four pets (May They Rest In Peace).

See www.poppyinkwell.com for happenings, the truth behind *The Shakespeare Rap* by William Brien, and exciting news about Book 3: *Bloodsuckers and Blunders*!